"Reading *We Imagined It Was Rain* is like entering a dream journal—
every sense is heightened and stretched, every memory expanded
and reassembled in the hopes of deciphering the past or surviving
the present. This collection reminds me of the very best writers of
contemporary rural stories: Jesmyn Ward, Bobbie Ann Mason, and
Wendell Berry. A keen eye for the truths of the human condition—as
well as a mastery of tone, detail, and imagery—make this writer one
to watch."

**—Z.Z. Packer, author of *Drinking Coffee Elsewhere***

"Essential stories from a terrific new voice. I read these eagerly and
wanted more. I feel the ghostly breeze of William Gay here, but
Siegrist is a big enough writer to blow past any forebear and carve
his own path. Just amazing."

**—Tom Franklin, *New York Times* bestselling author of
*The Tilted World***

"The stories in this book haunt the heart like ghosts. Siegrist's eye
for detail is so keen and surprising it feels visionary. Though set in
contemporary times, these are the oldest types of tales, of men and
women, of loss and love, almost ancient in their humanity yet made
bright for us again in the dark Tennessee woods. *We Imagined It Was
Rain* does not read like a new debut in southern literature but rather
as southern literature's new debut. Mark it down. Our children will
be reading Andrew Siegrist, longing for beauty in some future world,
well after we're gone. Mystic and earthbound, searching and wise;
this book is brilliant."

**—M.O. Walsh, *New York Times* bestselling author of
*The Big Door Prize***

"Andrew Siegrist's collection of stories is a deeply moving and spell-binding look at the human condition, Tennessee, and the heartbreak of daily life. His stories move toward depth and beauty, never flinching. There is a quiet power in every detail Siegrist draws attention to, and I knew I was in the hands of a brilliant writer who writes honestly, tenderly. This is a gorgeous debut full of heart and power."

**—Genevieve Hudson, author of *Boys of Alabama***

"With *We Imagined It Was Rain*, Andrew Siegrist establishes himself as a magician on the page. The stories in this collection transport its readers to the deep woods of Tennessee, where hearts are broken, where grief is fierce, and where humanity unequivocally abounds. From fireflies to baby snakes to a red lipstick kiss on the center of a forehead, Siegrist is a storyteller for whom nuance and detail still matter. This is a beautiful debut."

**—Hannah Pittard, author of *Visible Empire***

"There's much to be dazzled by in *We Imagined It Was Rain*—the startling images, the lean and lucid prose—but what I admire most is that Andrew Siegrist understands, more deeply than any young writer I've read in a long time, that the world remains a mysterious place, its magic grounded in the everyday dreamscapes of love and longing and loss. Somehow, Siegrist has conjured up the feel of magical realism without resorting to trickery or relying on the fantastic, and that, fellow readers, is a feat worthy of our very best attention."

**—Michael Knight, author of *Eveningland***

"These stories radiate with beauty and truth. The stories' scenes and characters are so vivid, I felt myself holding my breath while reading. Siegrist's imagery and details are first-rate; when you read these, you know you are in the hands of a talented, genuine storyteller."

**—Olivia Clare, author of *Disasters in the First World: Stories***

# WE IMAGINED IT WAS RAIN

# We Imagined It Was Rain

*Andrew Siegrist*

HUB CITY PRESS
SPARTANBURG, SC

Book Design: Meg Reid, Kate McMullen
Cover Image: © Hollie Chastain
Editor: Larissa Pienkowski
Copy editor: Stephanie Trott
Author photo: Meghan Aileen

## Library of Congress Cataloging-in-Publication Data

Names: Siegrist, Andrew, author.
Title: We imagined it was rain / Andrew Siegrist.
Description: Spartanburg, SC : Hub City Press, [2021]
Identifiers: LCCN 2021020599
ISBN 9781938235887 (trade paperback)
ISBN 9781938235894 (epub)
Subjects: LCGFT: Short stories.
Classification: LCC PS3619.I38395 W4 2021 | DDC 813/.6--dc23

LC record available at https://lccn.loc.gov/2021020599

Hub City Press gratefully acknowledges support from the National Endowment for the Arts,
the Amazon Literary Partnership, South Arts, and the South Carolina Arts Commission.

Manufactured in the United States of America

**HUB CITY PRESS**
186 W. Main Street
Spartanburg, SC 29306
864.577.9349 | www.hubcity.org

*For Celine and Frances*
*Yesterday. Today. And Tomorrow.*

**Take a mirror to the river. Then what.**

*—C.D. Wright*

# Contents

# Whittled Bone

Six months after Lane cut her hair and climbed out the bathroom window, Russell filled a fruit jar with dead wasps. He used tweezers to pick them up by their wings the night before, careful not to crumble their dry bodies as he lifted them from window sills and heat grates. It was early morning. His wife, Reesa, was still sleeping in Lane's bedroom with the bathroom light on. Russell stood at the kitchen counter, turning the pages in Lane's journal. He crossed through the entry dated April 14.

> *walked an empty house. no carpet no chairs. dead paper wasps in cupped hands.*
> *spiders spinning webs the color of blood.*

He had found the dream journal the day after she disappeared, taped to the underside of a dresser drawer. For six months, Russell busied himself bringing her dreams into the waking world. He gathered them and hid them in a dilapidated barn loft on the backside of his neighbor's property.

Russell left out the kitchen door holding the jar of wasps in one hand and a spray can of red paint in the other. He crossed the yard, stepped on a low line of barbed wire, and ducked through a fence on his way to the neighbor's barn. The woods were quiet except for the sound of waking birds and the dead leaves cracking beneath his feet. The tree limbs were bare, and Russell followed a deer trail from memory rather than sight.

The wooden rungs of the barn ladder were worn smooth from so many years of use. Russell wondered how long it had been abandoned. He climbed slow, careful not to drop the jar of wasps or dislodge the spray can in his back pocket. He imagined the sound of cattle breathing in the cold air, their nostrils exhaling clouds of wet smoke. He pictured them jostling for food, crowded bodies huddling around the salt licks, winter mud thick on the ground. Russell pulled himself up into the loft and dusted his hand on the seat of his pants. Old bridles hung from rusted nails. Opaque Mason jars lined the rafters and beams. When Russell first found them, some had been filled with bolts as thick as thumbs, and others, with missing lids, brimmed with leaked-in rain water. But Russell had cleaned them out and now used them to house the things his daughter had seen as she slept. In the middle of the loft, woven between two exposed beams, a spider web caught the light from the open loft door. Russell took the spray can from his back pocket and leaned in close enough that his breath disturbed the silk fibers.

When he stepped back and set the spray can on the ground, the smell of paint was thick in the air. In the budding light of morning, the spider web glowed red in the center of the barn. Russell picked out each wasp and placed it carefully on the web. They hung there, suspended, and when a slow wind blew, they shuddered for an instant, as if something in the blood web had shaken them awake.

"Lane," Russell said aloud.

He stayed in the barn loft until the sun glimpsed above a far hill. He closed her journal and climbed down the ladder. Frost still clung to the grass as he walked home alongside the cracked asphalt road. Log trucks passed without slowing down. When Russell heard them rumble at his back, he stepped farther into the roadside ditch.

Russell walked through the back door and into the kitchen. Reesa was at the sink staring out the window. She didn't turn around when he came into the room.

"Morning," he said.

She blew into her coffee.

He stopped and looked over her shoulder. Outside, a peacock pecked a stack of pane glass that was leaning against an outbuilding wall.

"Wish a coyote would get them," Russell said. "About tired of those birds. Shitting on the roof, standing at the windows looking in at me when I wake up."

"He thinks that's another bird in there," Reesa said. "Trying to peck it to death, his own reflection."

She turned and walked out of the kitchen, not looking up at Russell. He stayed watching the peacock peck the loose panes of glass. Reesa came back in carrying a duffle bag full of clothes.

"The light in her bathroom is burnt out," she said.

Russell turned and faced her. She had her eyes closed.

"And her pillows have forgotten her smell," she said.

Russell knew she was leaving.

For months they had prayed. They'd gone to church and taken communion. They accepted prayers. They stood holding candles amongst friends and neighbors. They walked the woods around their house with police, holding flashlights and looking for scraps of their daughter's clothes. For months they had told each other it would be okay, that Lane would come home and things would ease back to normal.

Then the police stopped coming by in the evenings. Cooked dinners were no longer left on the doorstep. The green ribbons that everyone in town had tied to their car antennas began to fray at the ends and come loose in the wind. Reesa started picking them out of rain gutters. She kept them in a shoe box in the trunk of her car.

At night, Reesa washed the dirty ribbons in Lane's sink. Russell would hear the pipes come to life in the walls as he flipped the pages of Lane's journal alone in his bedroom. Lane wrote of turtles active beneath frozen ponds. She dreamed that their house had a pulse and needed the windows to stay cracked so that it could breathe, even in winter. Russell sat atop a still-made bed for hours with cold air coming through the open windows and rustling the curtains, reading page after page.

Russell sat at the kitchen table, turning the pages of the journal and looking at all the dreams he'd crossed out, dreams he'd brought to life. He had flipped the breaker that morning, after his wife left, so that the house would be as still and silent as it was in the days after Lane went missing, when a summer storm took out the power. When he closed her journal, he heard a tree branch scrape across the glass of an upstairs window. The same sound he woke to that night—limb against glass—as his wife beat her balled fist against Lane's locked bathroom door, a door he later shouldered in. Behind it they found rain pooled beneath an open window and a braid of cut hair coiled in the sink.

Russell left the house. He passed the bare patch of earth where Reesa's car was usually parked and walked to the dry creek bed looking for bones. *Dreamt of cattle bones,* Lane had written, *whittled into stones and kept in the breast pocket of a worn out shirt.* Russell's shirt was red with patchworks of blue, duct tape at the elbows to keep the holes from showing.

He left the creek when he came upon a rundown, three-walled shed and a rusted silo that listed into the branches of a neighboring tree. In the hoof-cratered mud of the shed were three square salt licks, each furrowed in the center from so many hungry tongues.

Russell leaned his head through the open door of the silo, careful not to put weight against the tilted structure. Against the moss-covered ground lay a dozen crumpled beer cans and a spent condom. How many times had Lane snuck out and drunk beer with boys as he sat on the couch, unknowing, watching baseball games stretch into the late innings? He imagined her drunk and tangled up with someone who looked old enough to buy beer and drive his own car. Lane was thirteen and still slept with the bathroom light on. But Russell had already begun to see the woman in her, had noticed other men seeing it as well. He'd found pill bottles in the medicine cabinet, missing their pills. A pint of vodka in the freezer door. Welts on her neck that she swore were curling iron burns. Long-sleeved shirts, always long sleeves, even on the hottest days.

Russell placed both hands on the side of the silo and gave it all his strength. He pushed until the muscles in his back strained and threatened to tear. He wanted the thing to fall into a heap of twisted metal. The silo wouldn't give. How could something that looked so feeble be so strong? He pushed himself away and spat on the metal wall.

Behind the shed, Russell kicked at tall grass and leafless bushes until he found what he was looking for. Atop a large, flat rock were the bones of a cow. Its hide was tattered to almost nothing. Only a few patches of thin hair still clung to the sun-bleached bones. Russell toed them, listening to the dry sound they made against each other. He picked four ribs that he thought would be easiest to whittle into pebbles and tucked them into his waistband. He tightened his belt and walked toward the river.

A birch tree grew out over the current. Lane's tree. When she was still little, she would climb its branches to watch things drift beneath her. Deflated basketballs. Fishing bobbers. Driftwood shaped like things she knew. She'd call out to Russell whatever she thought the wood resembled, and, if it was something special, he'd dive in and drag it onto the bank. Tennessee, she'd shouted once as a broken one-by-six floated by. That night, he let Lane hold a palm sander, tight with both hands, as he moved the wood back and forth against the paper. He wet two rags with linseed oil, and they stained the wood together. When they finished, Russell hung the state in her room.

"Where are we?" she asked, pointing at the driftwood.

Russell found a sewing needle in the hall closet. He heated

its tip with a lighter and touched it to the wood. He tapped the burnt spot in the center of the state.

"There's where we are," he said.

Russell sat beside the river whittling bones into small round pebbles. When he finished, he stood and brushed the shavings from his lap. He circled the tree trunk to where Lane's initials were carved into the birch, the letters dark from age. Russell ran his finger over them. He took his knife and carved them deeper, where the wood was still bright.

Russell kept three of the bone pebbles in his breast pocket and put the rest in a Mason jar he would place beside the blood web. There were dozens of jars scattered about the loft. One jar contained nine dollars of pennies, each coin minted the year Lane was born. Russell placed the things that frightened him in a dark corner of the loft. Glass eyes removed from the heads of antique-store dolls. Knives with names written on the blades.

Walking back toward the barn, Russell remembered when Lane was young and liked to sit on his lap while he watched Braves games on TV. She'd ask him to play with her hair. He'd pin it back with paper clips and cotter pins. When he made a mess of things, she ran to the mirror and laughed. Reesa would hurry in with a brush and worry herself over the knots. One Sunday, at church, Lane bent down to lower the pew's kneeler and a cotter pin fell from her hair. Reesa picked it up, angry. Lane started laughing so hard Reesa had to pull her out of church and sit her in the back of the truck until the service let out.

With one hand on the loft ladder, Russell watched dust flitter down through the slanted glints of sunlight. He climbed slow, tightening his grip on the rungs of the ladder. When he pulled himself up into the loft, he heard a board creak, the sound of small footsteps. He turned and saw a young girl with bare feet holding a jar of feathers. They were the feathers of a rain owl sprouting from the open-mouthed jar like a vase of flowers.

He recognized the girl. Pastor Glover's daughter.

Russell took a step and the girl turned.

"It's okay," Russell said.

She was shorter than Lane. Her hair longer and blonder. Russell worried her feet were cold. She placed the jar back down next to a small pair of shoes and inside-out socks.

"I'm Juniper," she said. "June. I'm sorry."

Russell stepped closer and June stepped back.

"I know your daddy," Russell said. "You're not in trouble."

She took another step away from him.

"I have a girl. These things all around in here, she dreamed them." Russell moved forward slowly. "Saw them when she slept."

June looked around the room as she moved backward.

"I'm supposed to be home soon," she said.

"Do you ever remember your dreams?" Russell said.

June stood at the open loft door.

"You can look at hers." Russell said.

Russell saw her foot near the edge and reached for her elbow. She looked up at him, afraid. He tried to squeeze gently to let her know he wasn't dangerous. When he felt her twisting, pulling away from him, he let go. She stumbled and put a foot out to stop herself but was too close to the open loft door. She stepped out of the barn. Her body twisted, her arms reached for something to grab. She landed against a rotted mound of old hay and fell to the ground. The stale scent of hay dust rose and clouded the air.

"June," Russell said.

She rolled to her knees and gasped for breath. The bottoms of her bare feet were dirty.

"Stay still," Russell heard himself scream. "You're okay."

He tried to calm his voice.

When she stood, Russell picked up her shoes and socks and ran to the ladder.

June was gone. He saw a flash of her darting through the woods, clutching one arm against her chest.

Russell climbed atop the hay and sat with his back against the wall of the barn. Through distant trees he could see the sheen of the river. He leaned his head back and watched slow clouds drift by. A chicken hawk screeched high above him. He held June's shoes in one hand, her socks balled and tucked into the toes. He thought of her arms flailing as she fell and wished he had reached out and kept her safe from falling.

Lane is somewhere, he thought. Right now, she is somewhere.

Russell stood. He climbed up into the loft and sat with his legs hanging over the edge. He placed June's shoes on the wooden floor beside him. The sound of a car clattered down the rutted, dirt road. And then the engine shut off, a door opened and slammed shut.

"Someone in there?" a voice said from below.

"Up here," Russell said.

A police officer climbed the ladder, but Russell didn't turn around.

"That Russ?" the officer said. "What you doing in here?"

Russell recognized the voice, had listened to it so many nights, promising they were doing the best they could, that they'd bring Lane home safe and sound.

"Hell is this, Russ?"

Russell picked up June's shoes and stood. The officer poked the painted web.

"Don't," Russell said. "Please."

"This is bizarre, Russ."

"It's not what you think," Russell stuttered.

"Glover said someone threw June out the barn."

Russell looked at the officer and held out June's shoes.

"You know me," he said. "I'd never. She got scared. I didn't know she was up here."

The officer flicked his flashlight on and scanned the jars in the shadowed corners of the barn.

"I come here sometimes," Russell said. He looked around at the jars. He couldn't explain. "I never meant to hurt her."

"I doubt they'll press charges," the officer said. "They know what all you've been through. But you can't be here, Russ."

The officer led Russell to the loft ladder by the elbow.

"Come on. I'll take you home."

Russell sat in the front of the police car. He touched his breast pocket, pressed the whittled bones until he felt them hard against his ribs. The afternoon light was waning. With his face against the window, Russell could just barely see the spider web, still burning red as they pulled away.


Back home, Russell locked the door and busied himself cracking windows. Reesa's coffee mug was on the kitchen counter, the coffee long gone cold. Russell opened Lane's journal to the first page. She is somewhere, he thought.

A tree limb scraped an upstairs window as dusk shadows

crowded the house. He took off his shoes and felt the cold wood on his bare feet. He stood waiting, listening to the sound of the wind through the curtains, the still house taking deep breaths.

# Satellites

Their father planned to kill himself the day the UARS satellite was scheduled to fall from the sky. It was Saturday. Warm for that part of September. Outside the window, the sugar maple's leaves were blushing shades of red and beginning to congregate around the trunk in small patterns that threatened to scatter with sudden breeze.

Chelsea dropped out of her fall classes and moved home from Chattanooga. The first thing she had done was pull down the posters of punk bands she'd put up in high school. In their place, she tacked the constellation charts their father gave her for Christmas the year she learned that if you clap your hands in outer space, it will sound like nothing at all. She wore a pair of their mother's thick slippers around the house to keep her footsteps quiet and was often found in the closet, where their mother's clothes still hung, trying on lipstick that matched the color of that particular day's autumn.

Pinned to their parents' wall were NASA charts Jackson ordered the day their father sat them down at the kitchen table and told them his own orbit would soon be decommissioned. They listened and both ran fingertips across the underside of the table, feeling at knots of chewing gum hard as bent knuckles and tracing their own initials that had been scratched into the wood long before.

The charts were a mess of pencil marks calculating the exact time the UARS satellite would enter the mesosphere and begin to burn. Their father claimed he could tell the difference between a falling star and a dying satellite by the color of the flames.

Saturday morning. Their father woke himself with a coughing fit that started before dawn and didn't weaken until midmorning. The sheets on his bed were tucked tight to the mattress. The quilt their mother made from his old neckties was balled on a couch they'd moved into the bedroom after she died. Their father stood close to the window and his coughing fogged the glass. Between fits he traced lines through his own breath.

Chelsea cracked the door. Sunlight through the sugar maple colored the room, and she made a quick noise when she saw their father spit blood into the elbow of his dress shirt. Jackson stood at the door leaning his head against the jamb.

Their father spent his life looking up. Four telescopes sentried the house, one for each direction of the compass, and they rotated from one window to another throughout the year depending on the pattern of the stars. He worked as a house painter and volunteer firefighter and on Saturdays mailed letters to NASA, who never answered.

At his window on the day the UARS satellite would fall, he spoke as if they were not in the room at all. He said it was the last day of a long fight. His socks were on inside out. Chelsea pressed the quilt of old ties to her face.

"It still smells like her," she said. "Like both of you now."

Their father had combed his hair and buttoned his shirt as far as his neck would allow. Out the window, the sugar maple. A scattering of red leaves. The chain of the ceiling fan ticking a measured rhythm.

"I turned sixty-two the week she died," their father said. "She was determined to make her pecan chicken. Her old recipe. Birthday chicken."

Jackson took a step into the room and stopped.

"Her hair was almost gone. Wisps of it around the house were almost invisible until the light came in just right. There were sores on her arms that never seemed to heal or even scab over. For months, she'd been too weak to do much of anything. But that afternoon she heated the skillet, pulled bowls from shelves. I sat at the table and watched. Her skin was so thin I was afraid I could see all the way through her."

Their father turned the lock on the window and lifted it a few inches. Smells of cut grass and leaf fire. The sound of a small plane passing low overhead.

"She was nauseous and couldn't eat," their father said. "I cut my chicken into bites and as much as I wanted to eat it, to tell her it was as good as it had ever been, I could only look at the sores on her arms. The bruises and the dark veins."

Their father turned to them for the first time.

"She cleared all that uneaten food into the trash," he said. "I've never forgiven myself for that."

Chelsea stood and he wrapped his arms around her like he had when she was a child and woke late in the night, afraid of the things that only ever existed when storm wind rattled the shutters.

"I'm scared too, Chels," he said.

"You're still here, Dad," she said.

"It'll be okay, like falling asleep," he said. "Like wading into warm water."


For months, he'd rehearsed his plan every morning as Jackson cooked eggs and thick bacon. An overdose of opiates and alcohol results in the loss of consciousness, respiratory failure, and eventually death.

"Practice the pain," their father told Jackson. "When the doctor pressures the rib, try and look like you are hurt but not wanting to show it. Tell him you fell off a bike going too fast downhill. Tell him you waited a week before you scheduled the appointment."

Jackson put his hand against his side and thought of the blood on his father's shirt, he tried to mimic the look on his father's face when a fit began to take hold.

Jackson was unemployed, making enough money to fill the prescriptions by selling the things his father spent his life collecting. All of it boxed and stacked in the basement.

There were jewelry boxes filled with war pennies and Mercury dimes. Civil War tobacco pipes and mangled bullets their father had dug from the ground and kept wrapped in individual sandwich bags. Mason jars full with sea glass of every color imaginable.

In the corner of the basement was a summer camp trunk where Jackson kept the things he refused to sell. Inside was a rock their mother swore had been brought back from the moon. The best birthday present he'd ever received, their father said, pretending to believe her. Also, the hand mirror their parents bought at a flea market when the family was in Mentone, Alabama, for the Fourth of July. Jackson and Chelsea were put to bed after the fireworks, but their parents stayed on the porch drinking wine. Chelsea woke Jackson after midnight and the two of them tiptoed across the room and watched their parents through a cracked window. Their mother was on their father's lap, her cheek pressed against his cheek. She was holding the mirror so that both of their faces were framed.

"What do you see?" she said.

"The Queen of England."

She bit him on the ear.

"What do you see?" he said.

"The King of Spain."

They laughed and the kids fell asleep and in the morning there was a splash of red wine that had dried against the mirror glass.

The day their mother died, she called Jackson early in the morning and asked him to bring her a glass of water. He was living across town then, and when he hung up the phone he drove to a girlfriend's house instead. At the funeral, he told Chelsea she must have died thirsty. She said she didn't know exactly what he meant.

Jackson filled the prescriptions at different pharmacies in towns where he wouldn't be recognized. He emptied the bottles into a leather cup they used as kids to shake and scatter dice. The cup their mother once rolled straight sixes with as they ate ice cream in the attic while their father flung sprung mouse traps into the yard through a missing gable vent. It was summer and the ice cream melted fast and they licked their knuckles and knew everything was perfect then. Chelsea pretended to clap her hands without making a sound and whispered, *This is what it sounds like in space.*

Jackson scratched off the labels of the pill bottles before throwing them into a church dumpster. He kept the leather cup beneath his bathroom sink and stuffed it full with tissue to keep the pain pills dry from the sweating pipes.

Saturday afternoon. Their father held Chelsea and nodded to Jackson over her shoulder. A gesture Jackson knew meant the plan was to begin. The UARS satellite was losing speed, growing closer to the Earth's atmosphere. Their father coughed. It wouldn't be long before the sky lit bright and everything that was dark would come back into the light again. The satellite would burn to ash. A sizzle of embers landing against cool ocean water.

Jackson set the cup of pills on the sink counter. The faucet dripped at uneven intervals. Still stuck to the corner of the bathroom mirror was the Space Camp sticker they had put there the summer their father surprised them with a trip to Huntsville. Their mother drove the whole way and the three of them sat in the backseat together. Every few miles, he announced how much farther they had to go.

Half the sticker had been ripped off the night their father explained how one astronaut was always left behind. The others leave the shuttle to walk across the moon while one man stays in orbit. And at some point, when the shuttle is high above the far side of the moon, that man is farther from another human than anyone has been in the history of the world. Chelsea cried at this and tried to rip the Space Camp sticker from the mirror. Later, when she'd fallen asleep, their father glued it back. Ever since, you could see the rip where it had once been torn.

Chelsea stayed with their father a long time. Jackson didn't hear her padded footsteps when she came into the bathroom. She unspooled a handful of toilet paper and wiped the lipstick from her lips. A smear streaked her cheek. She looked down at the cup of pills, then at the sticker on the mirror.

"We can't," she said, touching the fractured line.

"His mind's made," Jackson said.

"Mine's not."

Their father coughed once from down the hall and then was quiet again.

Chelsea took two pills from the cup then offered it to Jackson. He shook his head.

She ate the pills with a swallow from the faucet.

"Doesn't matter, Chels. We could eat half of them and he'd still have enough to get it done."

"Can't be like this," she said, opening the medicine cabinet. There were boxes of Band-Aids decorated with superheroes and princesses still there from when they were children. Chelsea lifted boxes of allergy medication from the shelf and checked the expiration date.

Jackson squeezed past her and into the hall.

"I'll make him a drink," he said and was gone. His shoes loud on the wooden steps.

Chelsea stayed in the bathroom and popped the allergy pills from their foil wrappers and lined them on the sink. Ice clinked in a glass downstairs. Coughing from their parents' bedroom.

Chelsea ripped the corner off the Space Camp sticker just as she had years before. She touched the pattern of glue against the glass and put the torn piece in her pocket.

Jackson filled a Ziploc bag with ice and put the bottle of gin on the counter with an uncut lime. Saturday had always been the day their father drank. He'd fill a Styrofoam cup and mow the lawn in slow circles, passing over every inch twice. Their mother stood at the window and watched, smiling because she knew tomorrow he'd be sitting next to her in a church pew sweating out a hangover and praying that God forgive his small sins.

"Out there burning up like a son of a bitch," she said one afternoon. It was the only time they ever heard her cuss, and when he came back inside she had the shower running ice cold. The three of them stood outside the bathroom waiting for him to yip and holler as he stepped into the water.

Jackson came back upstairs with their father's drink, careful not to spill on the carpet. Chelsea closed the bathroom door behind her and handed him the dice cup. Toilet paper was stuffed into the mouth. Chelsea was chewing another pill.

"No more," Jackson said.

Chelsea swallowed and stuck out an empty tongue.

"I can feel the weight of my bones disappearing," she said.


It was late afternoon. Their father was three drinks in, standing at the kitchen sink and watching the faucet run. The clock above the oven read 6:08 p.m. Their father had predicted the UARS would fall at 9:34 p.m. CST. In one hand, he held a drink and the other was in his pocket. The water was warm, but he didn't touch it.

"Hook up the trailer, Jackson," he said. "I think we'll take the boat out."

Chelsea sat down on the couch and traded her house shoes for a pair of beach sandals their mother bought in Bay St. Louis, Mississippi, where the sun baked the sand so hot she couldn't make it from the car to the beach towel their father had spread so the hem touched a lazy tide.

"I never understood that," their father said, turning off the faucet. He turned it on again and left it running. "The pressure behind the water. Never did learn how that worked."

Chelsea held their father by the elbow on the way to the boat. Jackson backed the trailer to the porch so their father could step in without having to climb up or set down his drink. Their father directed Jackson with his free hand, motioning in a circle which way to turn the wheel. The sun was ducking behind the sugar maple and all those red leaves quivered like kaleidoscope fire in the breeze.

Their father sat in the captain's chair at the front of the boat and threw a stickbait crawdad against the back window of the truck. It stuck for a moment before falling into the bed and leaving behind a smudge of itself.

Chelsea stepped into the boat behind him holding the Ziploc bag of ice and the bottle of gin. The outline of a lime in the pocket of her jeans.

Their father doubled over in a fit but, before he was finished, raised his hand and waved Jackson off. Jackson put the truck in gear and rolled slow out the driveway. When their father sat upright, he didn't turn to watch the home he'd never see again retreat into the distance.

These backroad boat rides were something they had done

their whole lives. When they were young, their mother would ride in the boat with them as their father eased around the curves for hours at a time. Their mother always said she worried about them on the river, didn't trust the life jackets their father would buy and later return a few times every year. So they'd pretend those two-lane roads were swift current and throw hookless lures into the high branches of passing trees. They'd bet on whose line would grow tight and snap first. Chelsea knocked a squirrel from a tree once and their father reversed the boat until they saw the thing scamper off, alive.

Chelsea poured their father another drink and Jackson took a curve too fast. Some of the drink spilled and their father dried Chelsea's hand with the tail of his shirt.

They drove for hours, back and forth over the same familiar roads. Jackson watched the yellow lines and the rearview all at the same time. Chelsea was talking but he couldn't translate the movement of her lips. Their father smiled then broke into a fit. When he settled, Chelsea pulled two life jackets from the floor console. She buckled one around him, tightening the straps before putting one on herself. A passing car honked and their father lifted his glass in return.

Jackson sprayed the windshield washer and they both flinched when a mist of fluid jumped the cab of the truck. Their father covered his drink. Chelsea covered her eyes. Jackson imagined in that moment his father was remembering the splash of some long river full of largemouth the size of a grown man's thigh, a river that eventually emptied into the bay water of Mississippi, the bay where the sun beat sand so hot his wife couldn't cross it barefoot and his children played in the shallow water and didn't notice that she never once got in.

At her funeral, their father told them something about their mother they had never known. In her whole life, she had never learned to swim.

They parked the truck at the foot of Rabbit Hill, next to the barn where their father taught them how to shoot rifles, aiming at horse apples he balanced on fence posts. When shot, horse apples bleed thick white blood. Chelsea always aimed at the farthest ones, and when they'd all been knocked off, their father would walk out and juggle a few before setting them back where they belonged.

Their father unbuckled his life jacket and told Jackson to unhook the trailer.

"Here we anchor," he said, handing Chelsea the round metal anchor they'd never used before.

Chelsea lowered it into the grass and Jackson climbed into the boat.

Their father opened the floor console and dropped his life jacket in.

"When you were children," he said, "that's where we hid your Christmas presents."

Christmas mornings, they always woke to the sound of feet on the attic floor. Still dark out, he would climb up the pull-down ladder and stomp loud enough to shake the things they hung from the blades of their ceiling fans. Later, as they unwrapped gifts he'd ask, "Did you hear them? Did you hear them on the roof?"

In the boat, their father mouthed *Have you got them?* to Jackson.

Jackson put the leather dice cup into the cup holder of the captain's chair.

"Not yet," Chelsea said.

"No," their father said. "Not yet."

The sky was growing dark. Stars began to peek through, no bigger than grains of sand.

"She's falling tonight," their father said. "Seven thousand three hundred and fifteen days in orbit ends in a flash."

He was looking up, as if expecting at that moment the sky to light up in a brilliant streak of color and flame.

They watched with him as stars grew thicker. The night darker. Their father drank until they could hear it in his voice, swallowing pills when he thought they weren't looking. His children sat on the carpet floor of the boat, arms holding their own knees to their chests. And he above them in the captain's chair, watching the night sky for miracles.

"Take the truck," he said. "You can see the sky better up on the other side of Rabbit Hill."

Chelsea leaned into him and put her arms around his legs and Jackson stood, put both hands on his father's shoulders, and pressed his forehead against his father's. He said the few things he thought a father needed to say, and they said the few things they thought a father needed to hear. And they cried, and at some point later they realized they had all been crying for different reasons.

Chelsea jumped down and stood in the field with her back to the boat. She extended her arm and a firefly landed on her elbow and blinked once before it flew away. When it was gone, she climbed into the truck and pulled the door shut without making a sound. Jackson picked the toilet paper that had been in the dice cup from the floor of the boat and put it in his pocket. His father was beginning to sway in his seat.

"Any minute, Dad," Jackson said. "It'll be brighter than anything you've seen before."

Their father raised his head and looked at the sky for a moment before lowering it again and squeezing Jackson's arm.

"Brightest of all," he said.

Jackson closed the door and handed Chelsea the wad of toilet paper.

"Brought my own," she said, showing two fists full of tissue.

Chelsea cranked the engine and drove toward the far side of Rabbit Hill. They parked where the grass was still mowed short and the cold remnants of a bonfire lay atop the dead patch of earth they still used as a fire pit. As kids, their father had stoked the flames in that same spot and taught them the names of the constellations.

In the bed of the pickup, Chelsea and Jackson remembered those nights years ago when their father waved his hands across the sky tracing the shape the stars made. They lay on their backs naming as many constellations as they could and when they couldn't remember anymore they lay quiet and watched for satellites. There are thousands orbiting at any given time, but seeing one is a rare thing. Those pin pricks of light migrating across the night sky, bright and silent as any star.

Chelsea spotted the first one and traced its path with her pinky. Jackson watched until it was out of sight.

"When I was young," Chelsea said. "I thought satellites were stars moving faster than the rest."

Satellites don't stay in orbit forever and stars eventually burn out and go dark. But a star's light travels from so far away that by the time you see it go black, the fire has been snuffed a long time.

Chelsea stood and asked for a lighter.

"Got smokes?" Jackson said.

She shook her head and Jackson tapped the cab of the truck. Chelsea climbed back in and pressed the dashboard lighter. It clicked, and when she came back, its coil glowed red. Chelsea climbed on top of the truck's cab and lit a tissue on fire. She let it go and the wind took it further away than Jackson would have imagined. The flame whirled and dipped, rose again and fell. But it never hit the ground. It only lasted a few seconds and then burnt to nothing, a thin ash blown to dust. She stayed up there watching long after the flame was gone. Her feet made denting sounds on the metal roof.

When she came down, she touched the cigarette lighter to Jackson's hand. Warm but no longer hot enough to burn.

"Ready to go?" she said.

"About," he said.

He walked over to the fire ring and picked up a half-burnt log. Chelsea followed, and when he threw the log into the woods, she bent down and did the same. They continued this until their hands were black with ash, and when all the logs were gone, they knelt and raked the remaining coals into piles and threw handfuls into the dark where they could no longer see.

Out of breath and sweating, they sat atop that dead circle of earth. Their faces streaked black from where they'd wiped their tears. One Halloween, as children, their mother had burnt the tips of their school pencils and decorated their faces. They walked from house to house singing, *trick or treat, the coal miners hungry need candy to eat.* Their mother was at the window every time they passed by their house to empty candy from their pillow cases into the mailbox and head out in a new direction.

Chelsea put the flag up, and when they came home at the end of the night, all the candy was gone. Their mother blew Bazooka bubbles between sips of wine and told them the mailman picked it up and took it to coal country.

When they found their candy in the kitchen, the three of them sat cross-legged on the floor trading candy until they all threw up in the upstairs sink and slept together on the pullout couch without washing the soot from their faces.

Sitting in the fire pit on Rabbit Hill, Chelsea pressed her hand against Jackson's chest, leaving a shadow of her fingers on his white shirt. He touched her forehead and drew a Lenten cross.

Chelsea smiled a half-felt smile and stood.

They walked around Rabbit Hill until they were in sight of the boat.

From far away, their father was a dark shadow against the grass behind the boat. Chelsea took a few steps down the hill but Jackson stayed.

"We can't," he said.

She turned back to him. Her fists were balled and he could see tissue between her fingers.

"We need to go home and call someone to come get him."

Jackson pulled Chelsea back toward the truck.


The house was quiet except for the spill of the sink.

Chelsea went from room to room flipping on every light. Jackson looked through the viewfinder of the telescopes, but nothing in the black sky blazed. Later, he would learn the UARS satellite fell from orbit somewhere above the Pacific Ocean at eleven in the morning, in a different part of the world.

Jackson heard Chelsea in the bathroom. He knocked quiet.

"I'm okay," she said.

The door was cracked and Jackson could see her reflection in the mirror standing at the sink. He pushed the door open. Chelsea looked at him and took a step backward.

"I'm sorry," she said. "I couldn't, Jackson. I'm sorry."

In the sink were two discarded boxes of allergy medicine. The pain pills Jackson had been collecting since his father decided to take his own life were in the toilet. At the bottom of the bowl, the white pills had turned yellow as they dissolved.

Jackson flushed the toilet.

"He's going to kill us," he said.

"He'll be too hungover," Chelsea said.

"So he'll wake up soon," Jackson said. "What's he going to say?"

"Something."

"You should have told me."

"You would have tried to stop me," Chelsea said.

"I know."

"He'll be up soon," she said, filling a cup of water. "He'll need this."

Outside, a streetlamp flickered and a swarm of night bugs crowded the quiver of light. Everything else was still except for a possum scurrying across a telephone wire. Jackson wondered if there were any voices at that moment passing beneath the critter's feet and what words were being said so late when the rest of the world was asleep.

"We should go," Chelsea said. "Are you ready?"

"I don't know," Jackson said.

❉

As they neared the boat, the first thing Jackson noticed was that their father lowered the trolling motor the way he used to do when they'd sneak off to Marrowbone Creek and fish the shallow water. He was in the grass sleeping. His breathing was heavy. Jackson imagined him lowering the trolling motor and stepping on the pedal to listen to the blades spin one last time before climbing off the boat to die.

Jackson lifted the motor back onto the boat and stood above his father, listening to the heave of his breath. Headlights rounded the curve of Rabbit Hill and then stopped. Chelsea had gone to get the truck but parked and turned off the lights instead. The door swung open and she stepped out holding a red ember Jackson could hardly make out. The wind rustled and across his neck, Jackson felt the tickle of fishing line that had come unspooled from its reel.

Chelsea climbed onto the roof of the truck and lit another tissue. The flame moved in the breeze like a celebration. It grew, then shrunk and grew again before going out altogether. And then it was dark and Chelsea climbed back down and leaned into the truck to heat the lighter.

"Dad," Jackson said. "Dad, wake up."

Jackson bent and shook their father and pulled his ears the way their father used to do when they were kids and late for school. He tried to pull him up by the arm but couldn't. When Jackson lowered him back onto the grass, his eyes opened. He didn't jolt awake, didn't look around frantically as Jackson expected. His eyes were unfocused yet steady. He looked at Jackson after a few moments and tried to sit up. Jackson helped him and he sat there staring at his own hands.

"I was dreaming my hands couldn't touch nothing," he said

before a fit came on and he doubled over with his face so close to the grass he must have smelled the earth.

Chelsea was back on top of the truck. Their father's coughing eased and he sat up straight and took in as much breath as he could.

"Dad, can you see her?" Jackson pointed and their father tried to follow. "On this side of the hill, she's on top of the truck."

"Chelsea," he said.

She lit three tissues, one after the other. They moved about on currents of air, all following different paths. They burned quick and bright and when there was nothing left to see Jackson and his father stood.

Chelsea lit more, quick as she could, and before they realized it, there were so many fluttering and blazing against the black sky they couldn't keep count. Jackson's father let go of his shoulder and stepped forward. He raised one hand as if reaching out to pluck a flame from the sky. He turned his palm up and after all the fires were snuffed a fleck of ash landed on his thumb.

"I can't feel it," he said. "There's no weight at all."

He coughed and the ash disappeared.

"I never would have imagined it could be like this," he said.

They watched Chelsea come down the hill. She sparked her lighter once and then again. They waited for a flame to catch. For something to begin to burn.

# The Sound of a Father

The boy sits with elbows on the kitchen table, waiting for a match to strike, for the flame to touch the tip of his finger. His palms turned up as if cupped beneath cool water. Outside, dusk is fading. Evening bats swoop and rise and swoop again, like shadows caught in strange wind. The boy counts forty-three fireflies blinking out amongst the gloam. Lamps in the house are dulled, draped in newspaper. Gypsy moths flutter against the kitchen window.

"Deep breath," the boy's father says. "Count backward from ten."

His lungs tighten. He presses his hands together, afraid his father might see them tremble. It is August 1996. In three days, the boy will be ten years old.

He lets out a breath.

"Ten," he says. The word comes out like a question.

A book of matches in his father's hand.

The strike strip on the matchbox is made of sand, powdered glass, and red phosphorus. The match head is a combination of sulfur and potassium chlorate. The boy's father taught him this. The boy's father swallows fire on street corners for money.

The noise of the match scraping across the strike strip sounds like a seam in the world being ripped apart. Through the kitchen window, the glow of the fireflies' tepid flames. The match catches, his father's face glows behind it. The tip burns and quivers. The boy watches it reflect off the gel that covers his hands.

"Nine," the boy says.

His father touches the match to the boy's finger. His hands, still pressed together, catch fire.

"Eight."

He holds the flames. The tip of the fire burns red. Six hundred degrees. At the base, closest to his palm, it burns bright yellow, almost invisible. A color close to fourteen hundred degrees.

"Seven."

The boy looks at his father. His father stares only at the flames. The smell of lighter fluid burning. There is a wet towel limp against the table.

"Six."

The last number the boy counts. He turns his hands, fingertips toward the ceiling, and raises them to eye level. Flames ripple from every finger. His father drapes the towel. The sound of his fingers hissing. The boy is picked up, carried to the kitchen sink. He is too old to be carried. His father rinses his hands.

Pats them dry with paper towels, turning them over, checking for blistered skin. He puts the boy's fingertips close to his lips and inhales through his nose, whispering a quiet prayer, fearing the scent of something burnt.

"You're okay," his father says.

The boy looks out the window. Past the moths pattering against the pane glass. Past the flicker of the fireflies. The sky darker now. Dusklight, a promise growing quiet beyond the horizon.

The lights in the house are uncovered. Windows opened to the night air. On the kitchen table is a piece of paper with a crease down the middle worn so faint the boy worries it will come to pieces if touched. On the paper a few sentences are written in what the boy knows is his mother's handwriting. A date at the top, August 11, 1986. Ten years ago. The boy not yet born.

They had agreed for his tenth birthday the boy was old enough to see the pages of the diary his mother kept the days before he was born. Pages he knew were hidden, tucked between books his father shelved high in his closet.

And ten years old, his father said, is old enough to learn to handle fire. Learn to mix the gel that would keep his skin from burning. Learn to breathe, to steady his heartbeat. Watch the flames without thinking of the heat.

His father scoots the paper across the table. The boy closes his eyes.

"You read," the boy says.

The sound of the paper sliding back. Her words flat against the wooden table. His father holds it in front of his face with his hands cradled behind it so the two halves of the paper won't split apart.

"I remember this day," he says.

When his father begins to read, the boy imagines what his mother's voice might have sounded like.

*Ribbons hung from the ceiling fan. Blue and pink. We sit on the rug beneath them spinning. Closed eyes. The tickle of frayed ends on bare shoulders. I reach and take one, it pulls loose from the fan blade and gathers around my wrist. Blue ribbon. Baby boy. Your father says it doesn't work that way. I tell him we'll call you Grayson. At night when he thinks I'm asleep he puts his head against my stomach and tells you that if you are a girl he'll worry to the moon and back. If you're a boy, he'll teach you to be kind.*

*The doctor said you're healthy. He only showed pictures that would keep you a secret. We showed the pictures to a woman in the waiting room. She kissed my forehead. Healthy baby, she said. On the ride home, the windows down. Your father sang a made-up song.* Ten fingers, ten toes. Ten. Ten. Ten. Ten. Ten fingers, ten toes.

*In the driveway, a peacock feather. The colors of it are a song. A movement choreographed in water. I imagine your eyes already the color of something. Have you blinked yet, baby? What can you hear in there in the dark?*

*Inside, I find your father at the sink slicing tomatoes. I put my arms around him and he sets the knife on the counter. My cheek between his shoulder blades. The*

*smell of him, your father. Cinnamon and smoke. Worry*
*to the moon and back. Teach you to be kind.*
*Ten. Ten. Ten. Ten. Ten fingers, ten toes.*

His father folds the page and leaves it in front of the boy.
He circles the table and puts his hands on his son's shoulders.
Forehead against the top of the boy's head. The boy counts the
ticks of the living room fan. Thinks of ribbons, silent and spinning. His father leaves the room. The sound of the bathroom
door closing, the turn of the lock. And later, the sink still running longer than it should.

The boy touches the letter with each of his fingers and counts
to ten.

Alone in his room, the boy arranges creek pebbles on the floor.
Red ones around the bed. Brown pebbles line the baseboards
along the wall. He balances a white stone on the doorknob and
imagines waking in the dark, someone on the other side touching the brass handle. A hawk feather tucked beneath his pillow. Blades of dry grass taped to the window panes. The boy
listens to the sounds of his walls creaking against heavy wind.
He stands on his bed and draws fish on the ceiling before laying
down and falling asleep with the lights on.

The boy stands on the corner of Oak and Spring across from
where his father performs. There is a crowd gathering, watching
him spit flames against a restaurant window. Inside a young girl
touches the glass with the palm of her hand to see if it is hot.

The boy fingers the folded playing card in his pocket. As practiced, he dries his tongue with a napkin and puts the folded card into his mouth. He remembers not to swallow. Not to talk to anyone until it is over.

The boy walks quickly and takes his place somewhere near the front of the crowd. His father closes his fingers around a small flame, and when he opens his fist there is a penny on the palm of his hand. He spits a mouthful of cinnamon that explodes into fire. The crowd claps. The boy touches the corner of the folded card with his tongue. Inside the restaurant, the young girl cannot see the firebreather through the crowd. She begins to cry.

The firebreather asks for a volunteer and the boy raises his hand. He chooses a card at random from the deck. Seven of diamonds.

"Sign your initials," the firebreather says.

The boy shows the crowd.

The firebreather takes the card and threads a needle through it, suspending it from an invisible length of fishing line. He holds it in front of his face and lights a match. The young girl from inside the restaurant comes outside in her father's arms. Her face is still red and damp. The firebreather spits fire at the card until it catches and burns. The fishing line melts and the card floats away, nothing but cinder and ash.

The crowd waits. The boy breathes through his nose. The young girl wipes her eyes. Cars honk at the growing crowd. The firebreather bends and finds a flake of ash. He holds it under the boy's nose and asks him what it smells like. The boy breathes in and begins to cough. The firebreather holds out his hand. The boy coughs again and out of his mouth comes the seven of diamonds. His own initials written across the face.

The crowd roars. The boy touches the card with the tip of his finger. Wind scatters flecks of ash. The young girl stretches an open hand as one passes too far out of reach.

Moving through the crowd, the boy keeps his head down and ignores the people around him. The library is three blocks away. Six hundred and twenty-nine footsteps. The boy counts, careful not to step on the cracks in the sidewalk.

The librarians smile at him. Call him by his name. At a table in the corner, the boy opens a book and thumbs through the pages. Pictures of birds. Down the street his father turns a playing card into a thin sheet of ice that shatters on the ground, the shards begin to melt in the heat. The boy too far away to hear the sound of it breaking. Instead, he reads about the anatomy of male peacocks.

Their plumes are made of eye feathers and T feathers. Each consists of loose barbs and close-knit barbs, a white stem, a brown stem. They grow to over three feet in length. The plume is iridescent, appearing to change color depending on the angle at which it is seen. The eye pattern in the feather is a sequence of blue and green, dark purple and bronze. From behind, the peacock's feathers are uniformly brown.

The boy closes the book and puts his fingers in his ears. Tries to listen for the sound of the world before he was born. A car passes by on the street outside. The engine, the tires turning over asphalt. To the boy, none of it makes any sound at all.

That night, after his father rinses the fire gel from his hands, the boy holds a new page from his mother's diary, alone in his room. A jar of pennies emptied onto the bed. All minted the year he was born. He touches his thumb to a coin, feeling the date so small against the ridges of his fingertips. 1986. He balances a row of pennies on his forearm and traces around them with an eyeliner pencil he found in a makeup drawer his father never cleaned out. All the coins are tails up. He puts them in his mouth one at a time, touches the circles left behind on his skin, and tries to whistle.

He unfolds the paper and reads the words again.

*Minutes pass through the tree leaves without shaking them. The seconds settle into the grass. Your father and I walk barefoot toward the water. The sun moving beyond the hills. The memory of its light glowing the rain heavy clouds. He said I love you. He put a hand against my stomach and said it again. In our pockets we carry marbles. We carry wheat pennies and communion wafers. We throw all of it into the current. An eagle perched over the far bank. The sound of river against mud. The marbles sink. The pennies sink. The wafers float downriver until we lose sight of them. You'll hold our hands and feel this water against your ankles. Leaf fire far away. Silt between your toes. Will you touch a marble with the bottom of your foot? Will you take a penny from beneath the water and hide it in the corner of your mouth? Did the communion wafers make it all the way to the sea? Did ancient fish snap them up? The body of Christ given for you. The blood of the Lord. This river.*

Outside, the garage light comes on. The boy folds the page and leaves it on his bed. He crosses his room and stoppers the sink, spits the pennies into the bowl. The sound of them clattering and rolling against the porcelain. He turns the water on and leaves them there. His father is standing at his work bench in the garage, a briefcase open in front of him. The boy watches him through the bathroom window. The glass cool against the skin of his nose, silent breath fogging the pane.

The boy's father takes a hair brush out of the briefcase and smells it. The boy is too far away to see if there is hair gathered in the bristles. The metallic taste of the pennies lingers in his mouth. His father places the brush back into the case and takes out something small. He holds it between his thumb and forefinger, then slips it onto his pinky. A ring, the boy knows. His father holds the ringed finger in front of his face and with his other hand removes it. Both hands closed, tight fists. When his father opens them and shows his palms to no one, the ring is gone. He takes off his shoe and turns it upright, emptying the ring onto the work bench. He repeats the trick again and again. Finding the ring in different places each time. When he closes the briefcase, the boy imagines the sound of the locks clicking into place. His father opens the garage window. The boy takes a step back. The yard between them. Dark grass. The stone path grown thick with moss. His father tosses the ring out the window and turns off the garage light. The boy unstoppers the sink and listens to the water drain through the gathering of coins.

There are leaves pressed between two encyclopedias beneath the boy's bed. Orange and red. One leaf still holds a faint memory of green. The boy removes them and glues them to the ceiling above his bed. Leaves that won't ever lose their color. Leaves that won't ever fall. The fish he'd drawn there swim amongst them. Downstairs the screen door opens and slaps shut. Outside the grass already wet with dew. The ring, somewhere, silent. A trick not yet realized.

In the morning, the boy wakes to see his father circling the backyard in small steps, barefoot. The cuffs of his pants are damp. A thin cloud trails a plane overhead. The ring, somewhere, waiting to reappear itself.

When his father comes inside, the boy is at the kitchen table eating a bowl of dry cereal. He picks at it with his fingers. Crumbs are scattered. The boy notices the socks dangling from his father's back pocket. The television sounds from another room. Traffic report. Weather. Today will be a warm day. Storms late in the afternoon.

"What's the last thing?" the boy says. "Before I was born."

His father pulls out a chair but doesn't sit.

"We found a camera at a junk market," he says. "It was early in the morning. She hung it around her neck. We drove. Windows rolled down. The radio loud. She said, pull over, and we walked along a fence line toward the river."

His father pushed the chair back under the table and leaned his weight against the back of it.

"Pictures," he says. "She took pictures of an abandoned building missing its door. A footprint hardened in dry mud. I followed behind her. Near the river she bent down and picked a dandelion. Put it to her mouth but instead of blowing its petals she breathed in, inhaled the white hairs and began to cough.

"We traded the camera, both taking pictures as we walked. A small plane passed low overhead, and she wondered if the pilot was close enough to understand she was pregnant. We stood ankle deep in the current. I pressed the wrong button on the camera and the back of it opened. The film was exposed. The pictures ruined.

"Your mother laughed, unspooled the film and dropped it into the river. We watched the line of it snake downstream until it was out of sight."

"A footprint," the boy says. "An abandoned building."

"I remember a puddle," his father says. "And her bent down beside it, the camera raised to her eye. The puddled still rippling from a cardinal we'd scared off."

"What pictures did you take?"

"Every picture I took was of her."

Night. The sound of a coin dropped into a glass of water. The liquid turns red, then purple, then clear again and the penny is gone. His father picks up the glass, shakes it. Nothing rattles. He hands it to the boy. The boy touches the water. Holds it up to the light. His father takes it from him and drinks it in two swallows. When he opens his mouth the coin is waiting there on his tongue. The smell of coming rain heavy through the cracked kitchen window.

"Did she play the piano?" the boy says.

His father puts the coin of the table tails up.

"She would write songs," his father says. "At night. She liked to sit at the piano with her hands on the fallboard. She'd sit there a long time before beginning to play."

The boy takes the penny from the table and crosses the kitchen. A breeze rustles the tree leaves outside. Upstairs a branch scrapes a bedroom window. The boy turns on the faucet and holds the coin in the palm of his hand letting water pool there.

"What did she sing about?"

His father stands but doesn't take a step in any direction.

"Small songs," he says. "About a berry picked from a thorn bush. The scatter of crawdads beneath an upturned creek stone."

Water runs clear from the boy's hand. He dries the penny with the tail of his shirt.

"She had a favorite song," his father says. "I can't remember. There was a line about a footstep and the sound of ice beginning to crack."

The boy sets the penny on the window sill and flicks it out into the grass. The sound of footsteps. The weight of his father's hand on his shoulder.

"She would have sang to you," he says.

The boy turns the faucet off. Drips of water tapping the metal sink. A branch scraping a window. The penny alone in the grass. Silent.

The trick they are practicing is simple. The boy chooses a card from the deck, holds it for the crowd to see. His father spits a flame and the boy's hands catch fire. The card turns to ash. A glass of water, and the sizzle of the flames being extinguished. The crowd examines the boy's hands. Nothing burned, nothing blistered. The boy shakes their hands. After the crowd disperses, everyone, at some point, finds a seven of diamonds in their back pocket.

"Take a deep breath," his father says. Newspapers cover the lamps. The jar of fire gel opened on the kitchen table. The boy doesn't count backward from ten. His hands are lit. The scent of lighter fluid sharp in the air.

"She was holding a shed snake skin the day we met," his father says.

The boy moves his fingers, the flames obey. His father hands him a card.

"She was barefoot," his father says. "Hair wild from the wind. I was performing for a child's party. She was the summer nanny to the birthday girl. I snuck around back afterward and saw her sitting on the porch. *Dare me to?* she said putting the snake skin near her lips. *I'll kiss it for a quarter.*

"I flipped her a coin and she caught it. When she opened her hand it was gone. She bit that snake skin and let it dangle from her lips. Later we sat cross-legged in a field. A lightning bug crawled up her arm. The coin, she said, I felt it in my hand. Only an illusion, I said. I took her hand and pressed my thumb into her palm and when I took it away there was a small mound of ash. She blew it away and kissed me. Her lips tasted like dust."

The boy places his hands flat against the wet towel and his father folds it overtop them. The flames squelch.

"We're ready," his father says.


The boy's alarm goes off at midnight. His birthday. Ten years old. He stands in front of the bathroom mirror. Dark hair. A scar, from a bike accident, separating his right eyebrow in two. A boy afraid of the sound of breaking glass. A boy who collects caterpillars in Ball jars and waits for them to cocoon, who believes that shards of porcelain laid against the ground will scare away snakes. He touches the mirror. Often, he imagines his mother still alive. All this an illusion. An attic trunk opened, her in a white dress levitating out. The trail of the dress so long he never sees the end of it. I'm sorry, she says, and takes a bow.

Ten years old. He turns off the bathroom light. She would have woken early and made birthday breakfast, he thinks. Blueberry biscuits. Brought them to me in bed. Orange juice with cherries in it. She would have lit candles on the window sill, let the wax dry against the wood.

In the hall outside of his room, he stands with a hand against the wall. The silence of a world asleep. There are pages of his mother's journal in his back pocket, the stone from his door knob. The boy tiptoes down the hall. The attic ladder creaks as he pulls it down.

From beneath a pillow of thick pink insulation, the boy removes a pickle jar filled with fire gel, his father's recipe. The boy untwists the cap, sniffs the clear jelly. He dips his finger in. Touches the tip of his tongue.

Down the ladder. Across the house. The boy puts his ear to the keyhole of his father's door. Quiet. He turns the knob. The moon through the slats of the window blinds casts thin shadows across the bed. The boy can still taste the tip of his finger. He stands beside the bed and puts his hand on his father's elbow.

When his father wakes neither of them speak. The boy unfolds the pages from his pocket and lays them out across the bed. His father sits up, his back against the headboard, and turns on a lamp. They both squint at the light.

"I was dreaming we were swimming in the lake," his father says. "And everything smelled like lemons."

His father looked down at the papers spread around him.

The boy unscrews the lid of the gel jar and begins to cover each of his father's fingers. Each knuckle. He wipes his hands on the tail of his shirt and screws back the lid of the jar.

"There are no more pages?" the boy says.

His father looks at the papers on the bed in front of him. His hands held out in front of himself reflecting the lamplight. He shakes his head.

The boy turns off the lamp, strikes a match and touches it to his father's hand. Flames light the room.

"Then we'll start from the beginning again," the boy says.

He picks up the first page of his mother's diary and extends it to his father.

His father pulls his hands away.

"Only an illusion," the boy says.

His father reaches for the page and begins to read. The paper quickly catches fire. The words begin to wither. Soon there is nothing left but ash and flame.

The sound of a father and son reciting every word from memory.

# Nothing for the Journey

The boy's hands smelled like asphalt and the girl held them tight like she was afraid if the world kept spinning she'd lose her balance.

He'd hung their shoes from a trestle bridge and left them dangling above the water. They both walked slow in the dew-wet grass beside a road neither of them had ever been on before.

The boy took coins and acorn caps from his pockets and flicked them into the ditch, because you can't take nothing for the journey, he said. When he wasn't looking, the girl picked up a Mercury dime and closed it tight in her fist.

She didn't know his name. He had green eyes the color of a memory she couldn't place, and blonde hair cut short and uneven, like he'd done it himself in a room without mirrors. He spoke slow and smiled shy when he looked at her. She worried if he knew anything about her at all that smile would turn. That brightness in his eyes would dull and he'd see her the same way everyone else did.

So when he asked questions, she lied. Told him her skin was dark from Indian blood. Told him when she was in high school, she ran away from home and lived with her grandmother on a reservation in the mountains of North Carolina. Said she could braid bird feathers into patterns that would show the future, and that her grandmother gave her nicknames like Smooth Stone, Little Mouse, and Bone.

They ate breakfast in a diner before the sun came up. She had the word of the Lord tattooed across the back of her neck, and the boy traced each letter with his pinky finger and swore her skin was warmer there somehow. The girl scooted close to him and rested her head against his chest so she could feel the vibrations of his voice.

Tell me one true thing, she said. One thing you never told anyone, so it'll be just me and you that know it.

The boy's first pet was an imaginary friend named Pumpernickel. Pumpernickel was a sheep dog, had eyes two different colors, and would bark out small sentences the boy could understand when he was alone.

Pumpernickel was hit by a car on the boy's fifth birthday and was buried in the shade of a hemlock tree.

Never told anyone that? she said.

Promise, he said.

Cross your heart, she said. Hope to die.

He kissed her on the top of her head. It was summer and in summer her hair always smelled like rain. She put her head in his lap and stretched her legs across the vinyl booth. There was a scar running up her ankle and he asked for the story.

The truth? she said.

And he waited.

She'd been pregnant the night she saw lightning and snow at the same time. Her dad called it Coldthunder, and she walked out into it and listened to so much quiet be broken by the crack of strange electric blue light. The snow was thick on the ground and she climbed a tree to the high branches to see above it all. Didn't realize her hands had gone numb until she tried to climb down and lost her grip. Her dad laid her in the back of the car and drove to the hospital with her crooked leg raised on a stack of pillows. And that's where they learned about the baby. The doctors said if it had survived, she wouldn't have started showing for a couple weeks. Her dad said it was for the best, that she was only a child herself. On the drive home, the lightning had stopped and all around was a covering of white beneath dark sky.

The boy wasn't smiling, but that brightness was still in his eyes and, for a moment, the girl let herself believe he'd never looked at anyone like that before.

Does it still hurt? the boy said.

She covered the scar on her ankle with a napkin.

When bone breaks, she said, it grows stronger where it heals. Strong as iron.

The check came. She unfastened her necklace and laid it on the table. The necklace was silver. The shape of a feather.

He followed her outside and they watched through the window as the waitress put the necklace around her neck. Then they crossed the street to the bus station. He didn't ask where she was going.

She didn't tell him she was going home, that she'd called her father the night before for the first time in two years.

She stepped into the bus, squeezed down the aisle and into a seat by the window.

He stood outside and tossed parking lot gravel at the bus until she looked out.

Your name, he said. Your name.

When she spoke, her breath fogged the glass and he couldn't read her lips. She waited until the bus was far away. She traced her name through the cloud her breath had left against the window. A child stood on the seat in front of her and rested his chin on the seatback. She felt in her pocket for the Mercury dime she'd saved that morning. She handed the child the coin. The child put it in his mouth and raised a finger to his lips. She smiled and wiped the fog from the window. Nothing for the journey. Not even her own name.

Years later, when the boy dreamed, she'd be there walking the dew grass or sitting in a diner with her head against his chest. He would call her Smooth Stone or Little Mouse, and she would scatter bird feathers on the table, arranging them so that the future was something they didn't have to fear. And when he was awake, he'd watch for her, imagining her in front of him in line at the checkout counter in a grocery store somewhere. Or moving outside his kitchen window tapping the glass, as if meeting that way was something they had planned. Her hair would be longer, but still the smell of rain. And he would know to call her Bone. Bone, broken then healed. Bone so much stronger than iron.

# Heirloom

Cole took the last sack of peanuts from the pantry and opened the front door. A stretch of crows crowded the power line that ran from the street to Cole's cabin. When he stepped out into the yard, the birds came alive as if the electricity running beneath them had escaped its wire. They squawked and beat their wings against the morning air. Cole scattered the peanuts across a bare patch of dirt where a car must have once been parked. He watched the birds descend. Some took the peanuts in their beaks and flew away, others pecked at the dry shells and picked at the nuts inside.

A ground bird cocked its head in Cole's direction, a peanut shell hung from its mouth. Cole knew that crows could recognize human faces. He wondered if the birds at his old house were hungry. If they lingered in the tree behind that house and waited for a face they would never see again.

When the crows had finished, Cole walked barefoot down the gravel driveway. Atop a lone fencepost sat a child's hairclip next to an empty peanut shell. The hairclip was bent, the thin metal just beginning to rust.

Cole hadn't told anyone where he was going the day he packed his car and drove to the mountains. But every morning after he fed the crows, he walked to the mailbox and promised himself that if there were a letter inside addressed to him he'd keep it sealed, take it out to some forgotten part of the woods, and leave it to rot amongst the fallen leaves.

The mailbox was empty, the same as it had been every day since he'd moved to the cabin. Cole thought about placing the child's hairclip inside and raising the flag. He imagined the mailman taking the clip home with him and pinning back a child's hair. Cole pocketed it instead and walked back to the cabin. He noticed the hardness of his bare feet. How after months of walking the driveway each morning, he no longer winced at the gravel's jagged edges.

When he moved into the cabin, there had been a stack of postcards in the kitchen drawer not addressed to anyone in particular. Just the street name and the mailbox number. Cole had pinned them to the sheetrock above his desk because he liked the pictures. Far off places he'd never been. A church in Barcelona with the faces of saints shaped into its walls. Petra, the ancient city carved into the cliffs of desert stone. A world of snow stretching in every direction.

Cole wondered if another postcard would ever come.

Inside the house, he placed the hairclip in a shoebox that was half-full with things the crows had brought. Scraps of tinfoil, broken pieces of a mirror the size of fingerprints. Things that could fit into the mouths of birds.

Cole crossed the room and unpinned a postcard from above his desk. The house was quiet. Only the creaks of the floorboards when he walked, or the wind quivering the windows that were loose in their frames. On the backside of the postcard was a list of tools and materials. Craft wood. Teak oil. Brass knobs and hinges. Saws and chisels. Cole put the card in his pocket and laced his boots. Town was three miles away.

Cole entered the hardware store, and the smell of popcorn reminded him of roasting kernels in the kitchen and his son laughing from another room. A man wearing an orange hard hat with HARD WEAR written across it in white block letters sat on the checkout counter.

"What can we do for you?" the man said. He had a thick moustache and was stroking it with a painter's comb.

"Smells like popcorn," Cole said.

The man nodded at a machine against the side wall.

"For the kids," he said. "Keeps them from getting bored and disorganizing the nail buckets. Help yourself."

Cole shook his head and set the postcard on the counter.

"I need what's on this list," he said.

The man picked up the postcard.

"Have to send off for some of it," the man said, copying the items onto a yellow legal pad. "Come back in a couple days, and I'll have it for you."

Cole put the postcard in his pocket.

"Appreciate it," he said. He turned to leave, but stopped. "Wouldn't happen to know of any work, would you?"

"I might," the man said. "You got a strong back?"


Cole walked the shoulder of the road and imagined a car swerving toward him. The sound of screeching tires, then the impact of metal moving so fast it shatters bone. And then a split second of nothing before the asphalt dislodges a shoulder and burns away skin down to the muscle.

All around him were hemlock trees that swayed like clothesline sheets when the wind blew. He heard an engine growing louder.

A pickup truck slowed beside him, matched his speed. The woman driving looked to be in her late twenties, about his age. She had long, dark hair and skin that was darkened by the sun but not ruined by it.

"Where you walking to?" she said through the rolled-down window.

"Not far," Cole said.

"Hop in," she said.

"Appreciate it," Cole said. "But I'm that mailbox there."

Cole pointed.

The woman laughed. Her teeth were whiter than any teeth Cole had ever seen. He wanted her to stay like that, laughing, teeth bright against tan skin. She had a dandelion bloom tucked into the hair above her ear.

"Suit yourself," she said. And as she pulled away, Cole watched her rearview mirror to see if she would look back.

❉

Four days later, Cole walked back into town. A bell above the door rang when Cole entered the hardware store. His white shirt was dirty and heavy with sweat.

"Looks like they put you to work," the man behind the counter said. He'd gotten Cole a job replacing the fencing around the playground at the local elementary school.

"Again," Cole said, "I appreciate you helping me out."

The man nodded.

"Glad to do it," he said. "Now we got most of what you need." He bent down and brought out a shopping basket filled with things from Cole's list. "Some of it still ain't come in."

"That's okay," Cole said. "I'll just take what I can carry. Come back in a day or two."

Cole took out his wallet. The man raised a hand and shook his head.

"Pay up at the end of the month," he said.

The rain had already started when Cole left the hardware store. He felt the paper bag growing soggy and loose in his arms as he walked. A car horn blew from a nearby parking lot. Cole recognized the beat up truck. A hand extended out into the rain and waved him over. The truck's fender was bent and dented and littered with faded campaign stickers from elections that neither he nor the woman in the truck were old enough to remember.

"Ain't taking no for an answer," she said when Cole came up beside her door.

Cole didn't fight her this time. He threw the limp paper bag into the backseat of the truck and opened the passenger door.

"I'm soaking wet," he said.

"It's okay," she said. "This truck's seen worse."

Cole climbed in. The rain beat loud against the metal roof.

The woman pulled back onto the road and eased around the sharp curves, the windshield wipers fighting to keep up with the downpour.

"I'm Tia," she said.

Cole reached out his hand.

"Cole," he said.

Tia shook his hand then wiped hers on the leg of her pants.

"You been following me?" Cole said.

Tia laughed.

"I work at that boutique next to the hardware store," she said. "Got off and saw you standing there in the rain."

"Well," Cole said. "Thank you."

"What you doing with all that?" Tia said, reaching her arm into the backseat and rustling the bag Cole had bought at the hardware store.

"Building an ark," Cole said.

Tia's eyes cut over at him, but she didn't turn her head. A smile swelled on her face.

"Looks like you might need it," she said.

"Seems this storm is trying to stay a while," he said.

"There's owls that can smell rain coming days away," she said. "When I was a kid we lived near a lake and sometimes there'd be fish eggs in the rain. Wake up in the morning and watch the minnows flapping in the yard."

Cole told Tia a story he'd heard in school about a girl who lived in the mountains in east Tennessee.

"Her eyelashes grew in long braids down to her waist," he said. "In the spring, she'd look for sacred ground and bury pages of the Bible. She'd pray for rain. People would come to take pictures of what grew there."

"I bet it was beautiful," Tia said.

"I bet it wasn't true," Cole said.

"You know," Tia said, "every drop of water on earth has been here since the beginning of time."

She reached over and poked Cole's midsection.

"And that seventy percent of the human body is water. So that means seventy present of you has, at some point, been rain."

Cole didn't know if Tia had a screw loose or if she was just aware of all the magic still tucked into the creases of the world. Either way, he figured if she prayed to the falling rain, something would grow.

When they pulled into Cole's driveway, the rain had worsened and Tia was leaned over the steering wheel, the speedometer never breaking idle speed.

"You're welcome to stay on the porch and wait out the storm," Cole said.

Tia pulled up to Cole's cabin and shifted into park.

"Wouldn't even take a ride from a girl one day, and trying to lure her into his house the next." Tia shook her head and clicked her tongue.

Cole fought back a smile.

Tia cut the engine and looked over at Cole.

"Well, go on," she said. "Lure me."

Tia opened her door and stepped out into the rain.

Cole took his bag out from the backseat and ran to the porch. Tia was already standing there drying her face with her shirt tail.

"Oh, I'm sorry," she said as Cole emptied his things onto the porch. "You need some help with all that?"

"That'd been a nice offer a minute ago," Cole said.

Tia swatted Cole's forearm and rested her hand there for a second.

"Got any towels?" Tia said.

Cole hesitated. He didn't know how the cabin would feel with someone else in it.

Inside was bare. There was a mattress in the center of the cabin, quilts and sheets scattered about it. Books lined the walls in uneven stacks and were topped with coffee mugs and candy bar wrappers. Painter's paper hung in the doorway to the bathroom. The ladder that led to the loft was littered with dirty clothes.

"Don't go up there much?" Tia said.

Cole handed her a towel and a dry T-shirt.

"Found a dead rat up there when I first moved in," Cole said. "Kind of soured me on it."

"You read all these books?" Tia said.

"Not much else to do," Cole said. "I've got a computer, but no internet. Watched all the movies I brought with me after a few days living here."

Cole made a pot of coffee and told Tia about the postcards. His shirt hung down almost to her knees. Her wet shoes were next to the door and she walked on her tiptoes when she moved around the cabin.

She unpinned the postcards one at a time and turned them over to look at the pictures.

"Who you think sent them?" she said.

"I don't know," Cole said. "They're postmarked from around Chattanooga so they didn't come from where those pictures were taken. Found them in that drawer over there when I moved in, probably been here for years."

Tia flipped the cards over and read the writing on the backs.

"What're these instructions?"

"Some kind of box, I think," Cole said. "Figured I'd go ahead and start building it, see what it is."

Tia re-pinned the postcards, careful that the tacks went back through the original hole, with the pictures facing out.

"That's a church in Spain," Cole said, tapping a postcard. "They've been building it for over a hundred years."

Tia traced her finger over the spires.

"Looks like those drip castles you make at the beach," she said.

"Never been," Cole said.

"To Spain?"

"The ocean."

Tia took Cole's hand and looked at his palm as if she could see in the lines of his skin everywhere he'd ever been.

Cole told Tia about other postcards. About the architect, Gaudi, who built entire parks out of mosaic tiles.

"It's like he just woke up," Cole said, "and built whatever he saw in his dreams."

As Cole talked, Tia emptied the last of her coffee out an open window and refilled it with rain water that was dripping from the eaves. She said the moss on the roof was as good a filter as any and drank it down in three long swallows.

Cole shook his head.

"You were born about half wild, weren't you?" Cole said.

Tia reached the mug back through the window and filled it again. She handed it to Cole, and he sipped at it the way he'd sip something too hot to drink.

"It's good for you," Tia said.

She took Cole by the hand and pulled him toward the back door.

"Come on," she said.

Cole pulled free when Tia stepped off the porch and into the rain. She turned and held her arms out to her sides, the rain pooling in the palms of her hands.

"You know there is a coffin full of water buried in these woods," Tia said as she stood barefoot in the mud.

"Bullshit," Cole said. He was smiling, watching Tia move about the yard.

"It's true," she said. "This old man died and wanted his ashes to be scattered at sea. Said he wanted to be buried there and in his place told his family to fill his casket with ocean water. And that's what they did. You imagine that?"

"Sure can't."

"My daddy swears that if you stand on that man's grave you can smell the sea."

"Y'all been on the mountain too long," Cole said. "Lost your minds, that's what I think."

"You think there's a girl with braids for eyelashes out here, but can't be a coffin filled with seawater?"

"Never said I believed in her, just a story I used to hear."

Tia kicked puddle water at Cole.

"How you want to be buried?" she said.

"Never thought about it."

"Well, think about it."

"Just bury me regular, I guess."

Tia turned and looked out at the woods. Cole stayed on the porch.

"That or burn me up," he said.

"Sad, if you ask me," she said. "Those coffins now are made of metal, or wood with so much polish it won't ever rot. And they cremate so many people you never know whose ashes you have on your mantel. They just keep those fires running all the time and scoop out whatever ash is closest when the family comes asking."

"What's your way?"

"Plain wood box," she said. "Cut from wood around here. No polish, no nothing. I don't want to be stuck in there too long. I want to be part of the earth quick. Plant a tree over my grave and let its roots grow around my bones."

"What kind of tree?"

"Evergreen," she said. "With leaves that never fall."

That night, Tia slept on the mattress in the middle of the room. Cole hadn't asked her to stay. She'd taken one of his books and sat down on his mattress to read. Before long, she was asleep. Her damp clothes were in a pile on the kitchen table. Cole made a pallet on the floor beside her and listened to the slowing of her breath as she slept. He wasn't used to sleeping beside a living thing.

It was still dark when Cole woke. The mattress springs beside him creaked beneath Tia's movements. Rain was quiet on the roof. Cole felt her crawl off the bed and nestle in beside him.

"I'm cold," she said.

He buried his nose in her hair and smelled the scent the rain had left behind. Her breath was warm against his collar bone. He ran his hand over her ribs and tugged at the elastic band of her underwear.

"No," she whispered. "Just lay with me."

Cole lifted her shirt and cupped her chest. Tia kissed his neck and removed his hand, pulled her shirt back down.

"Take things slow," Tia said, sitting up and pulling a quilt around her shoulders.

"I didn't ask you to stay," Cole said, his voice flat and even.

"Didn't tell me to go, neither," Tia said.

Cole closed his eyes, and before falling back asleep, felt Tia roll away from him and climb back on the mattress.

Cole woke to the sound of a mug being set on the floor beside him. He could smell coffee and feel a cold breeze coming through an open window. It was morning but not yet bright outside.

Tia was crouched next to him.

"Why are you here?" she said.

"Thought this was the kind of place you could find some quiet."

"People in town talk," Tia said. "Think you're one of those guys like on TV, chops up his whole family and comes to the mountains to hide."

Tia was smiling. She blew on Cole's coffee and scooted it toward him.

"So, did you chop up your family?"

She pulled back Cole's blanket and pinched his arm.

"Did you chop them up?"

"Stop it," Cole shouted. "Don't talk about my family."

He pushed Tia's hand away and knocked over the mug of coffee.

"Jesus," Tia said. "I was kidding."

"And I didn't ask you to come here and kid me," Cole said. "Ask me why I'm here? This is my goddamn house. Why the hell are you here?"

Tia stood. She collected her things from the kitchen counter. Cole heard her moving around, but he lay back on the floor and stared at the wall. The door opened.

"They're probably right," Tia said. "You probably are some nut."

"Please," Cole said. "Just leave."

The door slammed shut. Cole waited until headlights washed across the walls and then were gone. The cabin was quiet again. Cole stood and turned on a lamp. He took a bag of peanuts from the pantry and went outside. He could just make out the sliver of the power line's empty silhouette. The rain had stopped, but clouds were still too thick for the sun to break through. Cole tore open the bag and scattered the peanuts across the wet ground, hoping to hear just one thing caw out from the dark and rupture the silence. Nothing rustled. Nothing stirred.


A few weeks passed, and Cole worked days digging post holes and putting up chain-link fencing. At night, he followed the instructions written on the backs of the postcards. He'd seen Tia passing in her truck a few times as he walked to and from town, her brake lights never lighting as she drove by, her hand never returning his wave.

When the box was almost finished, Cole stayed home from work. He woke up early and tightened brass hinges and drawer knobs smaller than the tip of his pinky finger. It looked like an oversized jewelry box with drawers of different sizes. He wet an old T-shirt and rubbed the box down with a final coat of oil. And as it dried, Cole walked to town.

Tia's truck was parked outside the boutique, and Cole leaned against it and waited for her to get off work.

"I finished it," he said when she came out. "No more postcard instructions to follow."

"How'd it turn out?"

"Not sure what it is, really," Cole said, as Tia climbed into her truck. "You're welcome to come see it."

"Can't," she said. "Got to run to the grocery."

"Don't want to give me a ride, do you?" he smiled.

Tia rolled her window down a few inches and cranked the engine.

"Sorry, Cole," she said.

Cole watched her drive away. He imagined the words of an apology. On the walk home, he kicked an empty beer can. He picked up a broken cassette tape and pulled out its ribbon. He was halfway home when she pulled up beside him, her passenger side full of grocery bags.

"Change your mind?" Cole said.

"Hop in the back."

Cole sat atop the wheel well in the bed of the truck. He watched Tia through the glass window. He remembered the smell of her hair after the rain. The touch of her breath on his skin. When they pulled into his driveway, he hopped out.

"Thanks," he said.

"No problem," she said. "Got to run."

The crows were frantic, moving about the power line.

"Want to see it?" Cole said.

"Can't stay," Tia said. "Need to get this stuff in the refrigerator."

"Ain't showed anybody yet," Cole said. "I was hoping you'd know what it is."

Tia shifted the truck into park. She got out and closed the door without a sound, leaned her weight into it until it clicked.

"Those crows are loud as hell," she said. "I don't know how you stand it."

"They're waiting for me to feed them."

"Really can't stay, Cole," Tia said.

"One second," Cole said. He ran into the house and came back out with a bag of peanuts. He handed it to Tia. She looked at the bag and reached it back to Cole.

"Just toss them," Cole said.

Tia opened the bag and dumped the peanuts in a pile at her feet and they walked back to her truck.

"I've got to go, Cole."

"Just watch."

The crows picked over the pile of peanuts and returned to the power line.

"Look," Cole said, pointing to a crow balanced on a fence post. The crow had something round in its mouth.

"What's it got?" Tia said.

The crow dropped the thing onto the fence post and it rolled off into the grass. The bird followed and took the thing in its beak. It dropped it back on the post again, this time steadying it with its beak before flying off.

Tia walked over and picked the thing from the post and turned back to Cole.

"It's a marble," she said.

"Come here," Cole said. "I want to show you something."

Cole led Tia into the cabin and flipped on the light. The finished box was on the kitchen table. The wood was dark and smooth and the lacquer reflected the lamplight.

"That's an heirloom box," Tia said. "My momma has one. Keeps passed-down things in it. My grandmother's rings. Family pictures. Locks of infants' hair."

Cole scooted a shoebox out from under the kitchen table with his foot and toed it open.

"They leave things," Cole said. "Those crows."

Tia lifted the box up and emptied it onto the workbench. There were dozens of small objects. She picked up a safety pin and a brass hinge-screw.

"I had a boy before I came here," Cole said. He picked up two beads and looked through their holes before setting them back on the table.

Tia was watching him pick things off the table. There were ball bearings and a bent paper clip. A broken button and bits of blue string. A wheat penny. Shards of colored glass.

"He'd drop bits of food in his car seat," Cole said. "When we'd get home from wherever we'd been, I'd take that seat out and dump out the crumbs. Cheerios or bits of chicken nugget. By the time he was two and walking around, a family of crows had taken to the tree in our backyard. They'd swoop down and pick over all the crumbs he left behind."

As Cole spoke, Tia pulled open the drawers of the heirloom chest and placed the objects inside, arranging them in rows by color and size. She closed each drawer without making a sound.

"He was tickled pink with those birds," Cole said. "Soon as he could say a few words, he'd ask me for a cup of peanuts so he could go out there and feed them. You wouldn't think it, but crows are smart. They'd see my boy come outside, and they'd start cawing. We started finding little things in his pockets and didn't know where he'd found them."

Cole closed his eyes and ran his fingers through his hair.

"A car hit him," Cole said. "Some high school kid. I remember him so well. Just sitting in the ditch beside the road crying. 'I'm sorry,' he kept saying. 'I was on my way to soccer practice, I was on my way to soccer practice.'"

Tia put a hand against Cole's neck. He opened his eyes. The crows outside were quiet, and Tia was looking at him.

Cole opened the drawers of the heirloom box and looked at the rows of objects neatly organized.

"Looks good," he said. "Like that was what it was meant for."

The child's hair clip was in the smallest drawer by itself. Cole took it out and pinned it in Tia's hair.

"Look good?" Tia said. She reached out and grabbed Cole's hand. "Come on," she said.

They walked out through the back door and into the dark woods. Branches scraping the skin of their arms. Heat bugs pulsed loudly from trees around them.

"Where we going?" he said.

Cole listened to the sound of their footsteps disturbing the dry leaves that carpeted the ground. Tia stopped, turned to Cole and smiled. Cole reached out and touched the paper bark of a cedar tree.

"Where are we?" he said.

"Take a breath," she said.

Cole breathed deep through his nose. And there, in the dark of the forest, he smelled it for the first time. The heavy scent of salt from a buried sea.

# Stormlight

**A**ddie was at the window when the power went. Her finger pressed against a crack where the pane glass had broken. The crack just big enough that it whistled when the storm wind blew.

Like breath, Addie said feeling it against the skin of her hand. The window sill was wet. Packing boxes littered the living room floor. Most of them still taped shut. Tate was opening them with a fishing knife looking for candles.

We'd already burnt them all, Addie said.

Tate crossed the room. Addie felt him behind her, his hands at her hips. All across the yard were pictures of clouds. She'd found them in a shoebox in the attic that morning and dropped them out an upstairs window. She wanted to see them below her, she said. Small reflections of the sky.

Tate ran his knuckles across the sill and Addie put them to her lips, tasting the rain that'd gotten through.

Someone's coming, Tate said. Through the trees.

Its her, Addie said. Lizbeth.

As children they had spent summers together. Addie came to her great aunt's as soon as school let out. Lizbeth stayed with her grandfather in a house nearby in the woods. It had been two decades, but Lizbeth reached over the fence and flipped the latch, letting herself into the backyard as if it hadn't been a day. She'd found Addie online. A quick message, came back for the summer. Decided to stay. Addie convinced Tate they could use a break. Get out of the city for a while.

Lizbeth held a magazine above her head, shielding her hair from the rain. Lightning lit and she bent and picked up a photograph. Thunder rolled in from a distance. Lizbeth wiped the picture on her pant leg and put it in her pocket.

She's not wearing shoes, Tate said.

It was still daytime but the sky was dim. Stormlight. Lizbeth knocked and Tate crossed the room. He turned the knob, then paused and looked back at Addie. She twirled her hand and bowed. Tate opened the door.

We figured your power had gone too, Lizbeth said, stepping into the house. We'd planned to come by earlier but this storm. I'm Lizbeth.

Tate shook her hand. Addie waved from across the room.

I've wanted to come in here all summer, Lizbeth said. I thought about checking the kitchen window.

Locks probably still broke, Addie said.

Lizbeth rolled up her magazine, cracked the door behind her, and tossed it onto the porch.

My husband, Jacob, is at home working on dinner, she said. Making enough for company.

We've got everything to unpack, Tate said.

We don't have candles, Addie said.

Can't unpack in the dark, Lizbeth said.

We've got wine, Addie said.

Lizbeth pretended to take a drag off a cigarette. She exhaled and flicked her finger at Addie. Addie toed out the imaginary ember.

Splendid, Lizbeth said in a fake accent. The house is still where it was. Addie remembers. Come whenever this rain lets up.

Addie remembered that as a child she always thought their house had smelled of fallen leaves. Lizbeth turned to go. Addie crossed the room and hugged her friend. Her cheek pressed and against the nape of Lizbeth's neck.

Can't believe it's been forever, Lizbeth said.

We've got an umbrella around here somewhere, Tate said, reaching for the knife on the kitchen counter.

Don't bother, Lizbeth said. I'm already swimming.

Addie watched Lizbeth walk back toward the trees. Tate dropped an old shirt on the floor and scooted it with his foot, mopping up where Lizbeth had stood barefoot, dripping. He opened the door. Her magazine was there, the pages growing swollen and heavy.

Her grandfather would sit by my great aunt's bed every night until she fell asleep, Addie said. Then he'd knock on my door and he and Lizbeth would walk home in the dark. He used to joke that he was the oldest boyfriend in the world.

Never wanted to move in together? Tate asked.

She wouldn't unless they were married, Addie said. He thought they were too far past doing something like that.

Lightning lit again. She looked at the photographs ruining in the rain. She held her breath and counted the seconds before she heard thunder.

Addie put two bottles of wine into a plastic grocery sack and followed Tate out the back door. They'd found a suit jacket in an upstairs closet. The style was out of date but Addie convinced him to wear it anyway. She laughed when he turned to wait for her.

Never see you dressed up, she said.

I'm wearing jeans, Tate said. He lifted a foot to show her the shoes she always told him should be thrown out.

Still, she said straightening the lapels of his jacket.

As they neared the woods Addie pointed at a rain owl perched on the branch of a birch tree.

Who cooks for you? Tate called.

I'd forgotten so much, Addie said. We used to climb the trees and throw acorns at the roof. Her grandfather would come out yelling at the squirrels.

The wine bottles rattled against each other as Addie navigated the woods.

Tate ran his hands against the wet bodies of trees as they passed. On their first date, years ago, she'd learned that he could identify any tree by the texture of its bark. It was the first detail about him that made her believe he was someone she could love.

There, Addie said.

The house, visible through the remaining trees. They counted seven candles, one lit in each of the windows.

Its bigger than I imagined, Tate said.

Smaller than I remember, Addie said.

Tate picked up an acorn and threw it. A small *plink* against the tin roof.

Squirrels. Addie mouthed the word. Less than a whisper.

Jacob answered the door holding a glass of wine and led them inside. There was a bottle half empty on the kitchen counter.

Everything's almost ready, he said turning to the stove. Glasses are above the sink. Lizbeth is drying her hair.

Tate poured two glasses. Jacob checked the oven. Addie offered to help, but he waved her away and refilled their glasses before they were empty.

Her grandfather wrote notes on our walls, Addie was saying when Lizbeth came down. Little reminders for my great aunt. She'd begun to forget things. We pretended not to notice.

The writing was so small, Lizbeth said. In the bathroom he wrote, 'Check the toothbrush, are the bristles already wet?'

I was so angry at my mother, Addie said. She flew down after the funeral alone. She painted over all the walls.

Jacob carried a plate of cheese out to the screened porch and the three of them followed. Battery-powered Christmas lights were strung from the ceiling. Lizbeth opened both bottles of wine at the same time.

So we can sample each, she said switching from red to white without rinsing the glass.

Addie slipped off her shoes and did the same. She liked the hint of pink the wine took, how it reflected the hundred small lights above them.

You wouldn't know it to look at him, Lizbeth said, but Jacob used to be a lawyer.

She tugged his beard.

Lawyers can have beards, Jacob said.

And that hair?

Jacob wore his hair in a ponytail that hung down his back.

He shook his head like a shampoo commercial.

Wore a shirt and tie every day before he we met, Lizbeth said.

We were living in Manhattan, Jacob said. It was lives ago.

His first wife was a very serious woman, Lizbeth said. Had to have the best. House, cars, wine.

Addie cheers'd her glass against an empty bottle.

We bought these at a gas station on our way in, she said.

I'll drink to that, Lizbeth said.

The two women clinked glasses.

Her first husband was a scuba instructor, Jacob said.

Search and rescue diver, Lizbeth said. And we were only dating.

Jacob stood and took the empty cheese plate back to the kitchen.

He's heard this all too many times, Lizbeth said. We lived together for a couple years, my ex and I. He'd get a call and just take off. Middle of the night, middle of dinner. Didn't matter. Wouldn't tell me anything about it.

She refilled her glass.

Only thing I knew about his job was that the water was always cold. He'd come home and run the shower so hot for so long the door would start to sweat.

Crime scenes? Tate said.

I'm sure, Lizbeth said. But again, never told me anything.

Kept a duffle by the door. Three air tanks buckled in the backseat of his car. Called them his obedient little children.

Lizbeth paused and traced her finger around the lip of her glass.

I always hated that, she said. Those tanks buckled in and that stupid joke.

Jacob came back with a platter. Baked trout with mushrooms over grits.

It's what we had lying around, he said.

The four of them served their plates and ate.

We went diving once, Addie said. On vacation. It was beautiful, about what you'd expect. I was worried the whole time the boat would leave us. Guess that's a different thing altogether though.

Moths were making quiet sounds against the screen of the porch.

You must have been curious, Tate said.

I'd read things in the paper and wonder, Lizbeth said. Leave work at work, is what he always said. But then one day I found an address. A slip of paper on the floor beside the bed. He'd just left. It was almost dark.

Lizbeth lit a cigarette off a candle on the table.

You went? Addie said.

She went, Jacob said.

Lizbeth blew smoke at the ceiling.

It wasn't far, she said. I knew the place. A reservoir we used to go to in the summer. It was next to a tower in a field the fire department used for training. We'd take a picnic and watch those boys carry bags of sand up and down that tower. Again and again. When it was over the fire engine would blow its horn and they'd shoot the hose up in the air. We'd wade to our waists with our arms stretched out waiting for that water to come down. I can still remember how it rippled across the surface. We imagined it was rain.

And that's where the body was, Jacob said.

Lizbeth dipped a finger into her wine and flicked it at him.

I never saw the body, she said. There's a road that goes up to a lookout above the reservoir. A little turn out where you can park and look down at the water. I went there and watched. It was late. I could see his dive light moving slow in the water. There were two cop cars parked and an ambulance. The ambulance lights were going, but the siren was off. Just those red and white lights flashing in silence over everything. The cops were leaning against their cars smoking, using one cigarette to light the next. The ambulance driver was standing on the roof of his truck watching the water. I was there for an hour or so when my ex's dive light went out. I thought I'd just lost track of it, but it was gone. No light at all in that water except those red and white lights reflecting across the surface. I heard the ambulance driver shout down at the cops and they all dropped their cigarettes. Stepped them out. The driver climbed down and turned off the ambulance. Everything was dark, and quiet. It was like the moment in a movie when you know something's coming. You tell yourself it's coming but you know it's going to scare you anyway. I wanted to run down there and crank up that ambulance and drive right into the water, lights and sirens and everything. It couldn't have lasted more than a few seconds. But it felt long enough for the whole world to change.

It sounds so, Addie paused. She reached and felt the heat coming off the candle flame. Lonely, she said.

But then his light came back on, Lizbeth said. He raised it out of the water and flicked it back and forth. The ambulance came back on and everything was washed over again in those red and white lights. I couldn't stay there for what would happen next. The last thing I saw before I got in the car was those cops lighting new cigarettes.

You never told him, Addie said.

I was in bed when he got home, Lizbeth said. Heard him get in the shower. I moved to the couch, couldn't stand the thought of him beside me, reaching beneath the covers and touching my hand. The idea of him under that water, in the dark and what was there next to him that he couldn't see for those few seconds. I've never been able to understand it. Being in bed with him at that moment seemed like the loneliest place in the world.

No one spoke for a few minutes. Lizbeth finished her cigarette. Jacob cleared the table. Candles burned down to stumps. Rain started up again against the tin roof. Addie thought of the owl perched in the birch. Tate reached for a cigarette. He'd quit years ago. Addie touched his arm. He left it between his lips unlit.

I remember as a child standing next to my mother at a flower stand, Tate said. I couldn't have been more than five or six. First real memory I have. It was just a folding table someone had set up in a gravel lot. My mother was buying roses for a party. White roses. I remember the man selling flowers made a comment about the roses matching the color of her dress. It must have been Sunday. I was pressing my thumb into the soil of the potted plants beneath the table and touching the tip of my finger to my tongue. Across the street a man came out from behind a building and stopped in a small patch of grass. Above him a single bird was perched on a telephone wire. The man was looking down at the shadow of the bird. He turned and saw me watching. He took a red string from his pocket and dangled it so I could see. He bent and tied the string to a blade of grass where the bird's shadow was. I remember he had trouble standing. My mother laughed at something I hadn't heard. The man across the street clapped his hands and the bird flew away. He turned back toward us. He wasn't smiling. In my memory he's very old. My mother touched my shoulder. The man walked away. In the car, I looked back out the window, I imagined that string fluttering off, tied to the shadow of a feather. But it was still there limp against the grass. The man and the bird were gone.

Tate slipped the cigarette back into its pack.

You've never told me that, Addie said.

I hadn't thought about it in years, Tate said.

Well I don't understand any of this, Jacob said. Maybe it's the wine.

The four of them finished their glasses. They listened to the rain.

Tate stood. Lizbeth reached over and took Addie's hand. She kissed her knuckles.

Thanks for everything, Tate said. Really.

Jacob put his hands together in front of his chin. Lizbeth led them to the door.

Outside the rain was cool against the skin of Addie's arms. Tate put his coat around her shoulders. She put her hand in the pocket and felt the sugared texture of a candy orange slice. She remembered Lizbeth's grandfather was diabetic. They heard the door close behind them as they walked toward the woods. Tate reached out and touched the bark of a tree.

Birch, he whispered.

And then, in a moment of brilliance, they were aware of their own shadows. They stopped and turned. The porch light was on. They could see through the windows that other lights were on as well.

Power's back, Tate said.

Addie took his hand and they watched. Jacob was going room to room blowing out the candles lit on the window sills. Small wisps of smoke. He brought in the glasses from the porch, two in each hand and put them in the sink. He turned on the water. Addie wondered if it was warm.

Upstairs they saw Lizbeth standing in front of a mirror. A picture was tucked into the frame. Too far away to see the image. Addie prayed for clouds. She wondered if the window was locked. Lizbeth took off her dress. Tate turned, but Addie watched. Lizbeth put her hand out and touched the reflection of her own face.

# Shinebone

Shinebone tucked hawk feathers into the laces of his boots and lit a cigarette. He had been scared of snakes ever since he'd seen his brother's arm swell up from a cottonmouth bite when they were kids. He figured if they smelled a hawk coming, they'd stay coiled up in their holes. It was early morning before dawn, and Shinebone stood on his porch listening. It was the hour of silence. He smoked down to the filter and flicked the butt into a lidless Styrofoam cooler that was in the yard. It was half full of month-old rain and bloated cigarettes and he knew the grass beneath it was dead. He and Clint both smoked Marlboros. Shinebone smoked Reds and would joke that he must have been a lousy parent to raise a boy that smoked 27s. But now Clint was dead, and there were still a couple 27s somewhere in the cooler. Shinebone couldn't bring himself to clean it out.

He stepped off the porch and headed toward the woods. He wanted a drink. A quick nip to warm the back of his throat and quiet the thoughts in his head. Not today, he told himself. Even in the dark, he could make out the shortcut path that led to the neighbor's trailer. The woods were quiet around him. Birds still sleeping. Possums and coons done scavenging for the night. When he got to the dry creek bed, he stopped. He knelt and gathered a handful of dust. Millions of years of rock and animal bone crumbled to sediment. Clint'd told him that. As a kid, Clint had kept a box of fossil stones beneath his bed. Shinebone would take him down to the creek to hunt for them. Clint would flip the stones and check their bellies for the outline of ancient shells. Shinebone taught Clint how to lift the rock in case there was a snake underneath it. Always lift the edge that is farthest from you, keeping the rock between you and whatever is sleeping beneath it. As a teenager, Clint said he was going to go to college to study geology. Instead, he dropped out after his junior year of high school and never left the mountain. Never would.

Shinebone wiped his hands clean on his pant leg and crossed the creek bed. Day was beginning to burn at the horizon, an ember light slowly warming. Shinebone bent at the neighbor's mailbox and picked up some driveway gravel. He circled to the back of a hard-worn trailer and tossed a rock gently against the boy's window.

As a kid Shinebone heard stories about a woman at the foot of the mountain that caused miracles by praying to God and floating candles downriver, out toward the sea. When they released Clint from Brushy Mountain, Shinebone started paying a neighbor boy ten dollars a couple times a week to climb an old oak tree and burn candles in the highest branches. Shinebone hadn't prayed in fifty years, figured there was no use starting now. God didn't keep an ear open for people that'd done the things Shinebone had done. But he burned those candles anyway, always at dawn, and hoped his son would straighten out, hoped for a miracle.

After three rocks, the boy slid his window open and gestured with his hand for Shinebone to wait a second. A moment later the trailer door opened, and the boy came out carrying his boots. He sat down on a cinder-block step with chipped-off corners and laced up his boots.

"When's your daddy getting out?" Shinebone said.

"They got him up for parole in eighteen months."

"My boy was in there for a bit."

"He out now?"

Shinebone nodded. He had never talked to the boy about Clint, never told him why he burned those candles. Ten dollars to climb and keep quiet, Shinebone had told him the first morning. He couldn't have explained it anyhow. Burning candles to keep his grown son safe. Didn't make any sense, not even to him. But he had to do something, and he had kept at it even when it was clear that Clint was beyond saving.

The boy stood up. "Where's the stuff?" he said.

"We ain't going down there no more," Shinebone said.

"Then what'd you get me up for?"

Shinebone reached into his pocket and handed the boy five twenty-dollar bills, tightly folded.

"What's this?" the boy said.

Shinebone tossed the gravel he was still holding back into the driveway. "I'll be around from time to time," he said. "To check up on you."

The boy and Shinebone both looked at the fold of money, then back at each other.

"I won't waste my money if I hear you've been finding trouble," Shinebone said.

The boy put the money in his pocket.

"All right then," Shinebone said, turning to leave.

"Thank you," the boy called out.

Shinebone kept walking.

The last time Shinebone saw Clint, he had come by looking for money. Shinebone told him he couldn't help him. Clint said he had figured as much but had to check anyway. He only stayed long enough to finish a beer he'd brought with him and a cigarette. It was almost dusk. No stars visible yet, but a sliver of crescent moon. Clint got in his truck and rolled the window down.

"Ever heard the Grundy County mating call?" Clint asked as he pulled a pill bottle from his breast pocket.

Shinebone tried to force a smile but couldn't. He sipped his coffee. Clint had been telling the same joke since he got out of prison. Shinebone wanted to tell Clint to flush those pills and straighten up, but Clint knew all the old stories about his father and wouldn't listen to a word of advice from a man who'd already done the things he was doing. Shinebone wished Clint would hide those bottles from him at least, like he used to do. But since he'd been out, he'd treated Shinebone less and less like a father. Even called him Shine like everyone else.

Clint shook the pill bottle. The pills clattered loudly against the plastic. "Grundy County mating call," he shouted.

He laughed and put the truck in gear.

That bottle sounded more like a rattler to Shinebone. A mean snake with a mouthful of poison, quick to strike at anything that moved past it.

When he got home from the neighbor's, it was full morning. His yard was wet with dew. He stood outside, not wanting to go in. Today he was scheduled to identify the body. Opening the back door would put him one step closer. He stood and listened to the morning birds test their sleepy voices. Dogs barked at truck engines starting. Shinebone went inside.

He buttoned up his shirt from the bottom, misaligned the holes, and had to start over. He fumbled at his tie, and when he finally tied it right, it didn't even reach his belly button. Shinebone looked at himself in the mirror. His sleeves came down to his knuckles, pant legs touched the floor. Just one sip and all of this would start to ease away. He walked into the kitchen and took the jar from beneath the sink. He'd kept it there for the last twenty years and never opened it. When he felt that thirst, he'd take out the jar and feel the weight of it, just to know he could if he needed to. He held it up to the light and slapped it. High-proof bubbles formed on the surface. Not today, he thought.

In his truck, Shinebone turned on the radio and listened to the weather. Rain was predicted to come in after midnight. He turned the radio off and rolled down his window. He felt the wind strong against his palm. He thought of Clint coming home from first grade with plans to catch fish with a kite. They had taught him in school that clouds are made from water sucked up from rivers and oceans. Clint's face lit up when he told this to Shinebone.

"There must be a thousand fish up there," he said. "Just like the ones we caught in Uncle Fez's lake."

Clint spent the rest of the afternoon tying rusty fish hooks to the kite's string and trying to fly it high enough to make a catch. When the wind died down, the kite got caught in a tree limb, and Clint threw rocks at it until the sun went down.

Shinebone parked in front of the coroner's office and turned off the engine. He lit a cigarette. He tried to take the whole thing down in one long pull, but he started coughing spit all over the steering wheel. A mother and son passed by on the sidewalk. Shinebone held up a hand to tell them he was okay. They hurried by and averted their eyes. He wasn't okay. They could see that. He tossed the cigarette into the parking lot and went to the door. He saw his reflection in the dark glass. He'd forgotten to comb his hair. The knot of his tie was crooked. His suit was too big. The skin beneath his eyes was wrinkled and drooping. He went inside.

They led Shinebone into a room bright with a light so white it seemed almost blue. The stainless steel countertops were clean and empty. The floor made squeaking sound beneath his shoes. All the drawers were shut, cabinet doors closed. Everything had been put away, everything except for Clint.

A man whose name he had forgotten led him by the elbow to the side of a table. Clint was covered by a sheet.

"Ready?" the coroner said.

Shinebone nodded.

The man pulled the sheet down just enough to reveal Clint's face and the tops of his shoulders. His eyes were closed. His skin pale and cold, as if a light had been switched off behind it. His hair dark brown and just long enough for it to be worn messy. Shinebone noted the scar that separated Clint's eyebrow. He remembered the cut was too close to the optical nerve, so the doctor couldn't give Clint Novocaine. Clint was eleven years old. The doctor strapped him to the table in something like a straightjacket to keep him still. Shinebone held his hand as the doctor sewed his eyebrow shut. Clint didn't even squeeze his hand. Shinebone had wished he had, wished he'd squeezed hard so Shinebone could share some of the pain.

Shinebone wanted to cover his son's body back up and carry it out. Clint wouldn't have wanted to be in there. He didn't like places like this, so neat and sterile. Clint liked weeds that came up through the sidewalk, kitchen sinks full of dishes, jeans with holes at the knees. Shinebone wondered if he still had the strength to sling Clint over his shoulder. When Clint was little Shinebone would call out *Bedtime for Bonzo* every night before bed. Clint would run around the living room begging for thirty more minutes. When Shinebone caught him he'd shout out *Sack of potatoes* and sling Clint over his shoulder, carrying him to bed.

"Would you like a moment?" the coroner asked.

"No," Shinebone said. *I'd like a drink*, he thought.

The coroner covered Clint's face and handed Shinebone a one-gallon Ziploc bag. "Everything that was on him," the man said.

Shinebone took the bag without going through its contents. He signed some papers and left the building. He breathed deep, relieved to be outside.

Shinebone took off the suit and laid it on the bed. He stood looking at it, knowing the next time he wore a suit he would be lying in his own casket. He got a wire hanger from the closet and hung the suit on the nail he'd half-driven into the bathroom door. He'd been hanging things from that nail since before Clint was born. Twenty-seven years, and it wasn't going anywhere anytime soon.

In the kitchen, Shinebone put on a pot of coffee and waited. Through the window above the sink he watched the sun struggle to keep the world alight. Only a sliver still visible above the tree line. When his coffee was ready, he took it to the porch and lit a cigarette. He smoked it down and listened to the paper sizzle when he took a deep drag. When he finished, he flicked it into the cooler and heard the sound of the ember tip hiss as it hit the water, all its heat gone in an instant. He set his coffee down, unsipped, and walked to the cooler. The water was murky and crowded with cigarettes and dead leaves. An insect floated belly up, legs kicking for something to grab onto. Shinebone wondered if Clint had fought, had kicked and struggled to grab onto something as life slipped him, but with so many pills in his stomach he'd probably just fallen asleep.

Shinebone tipped the cooler over with the toe of his boot. The water spread across the yard and pooled, only for a second, before soaking into the ground. Soggy cigarette butts littered the grass. The insect righted itself and scampered away. Shinebone went to the garage and came back with a shovel and a rake. He carefully dug up a clump of grass and set it aside. Daylight was no longer on the horizon, but he could still make out the cigarettes against the dark blanket of grass. He dug two shovelfuls of dirt from the hole and raked all the cigarette butts into it. He filled the hole and returned the grass clump, tamping it down with the heel of his boot. He imagined what noises could be heard underground. Blind creatures tunneling their way through the darkness, scratching roots as they passed. Footprints from the above ground world, like slow rolling thunder.

Shinebone unwound the garden hose and washed the cooler out. A brown stain marked the level the water had been and no matter how much he scrubbed the stain remained. He placed the cooler back where it had been. He knew what he was going to do now. He was going to leave it there, let it fill back up with rain. But this time he would keep it clean. He would buy a goldfish net and skim the water each morning. Clean as tap water. He would watch storm clouds come in slow and unleash water that had evaporated from rivers and oceans halfway across the world. He would drink coffee on the porch, watching the cooler fill, watching till the water rose up and spilled over the edges.

Shinebone returned to the kitchen and took the liquor jar from beneath the sink. He uncapped it and breathed in the fumes. The scent burnt his throat, made his eyes threaten to water. Not today, he told himself. He poured the liquor down the drain and turned on the faucet to rid the sink of the smell. He rinsed the jar. This was the first time in his life that he was living in a dry house. From that moment on when he felt the thirst tightening its fist, he'd fill the jar with storm water and drink. Jar after jar, until his belly was tight. But tonight the cooler was empty, tonight he would sit on the porch and wait for the rain.

# Rainpainting

The summer we lived with Dad, there was a neighbor whose voice we never heard. We'd see him walking through the woods, fingers brushing the bark of trees. Or rustling the leaves of bushes, collecting berries in a paper sack. Sometime he crouched in the creek bed and picked red pebbles from the cool water.

He moved slow. Always quiet. And often stopped as if listening to things we couldn't hear, like roots growing deep beneath him. The crack of a bird's egg in a high-up nest.

Once we drove by him on the gravel road near our house. He stepped into the ditch and waited for us to pass. Dad raised two fingers from the steering wheel, and the man lifted his hand to his forehead. Waving hello or shading his eyes from the sun, we couldn't tell.

"The Rainpainter," Dad said, watching the rearview mirror.

When we asked what he meant, he told us he'd show us, but we'd have to wait.

We stayed up late that night making up stories. The Rainpainter standing beneath a heavy sky, wetting his brush with storm water. Slashing at a canvas until something evil took shape. We listened with our ears pressed against the window for some promise of rain to break loose from the sky, some spark to waken the dark world. And if it had, we'd have been afraid to open our eyes, afraid the stories we told were true.

The next morning, he walked past our house carrying a stack of folded sheets.

"What's he doing?" we said.

"Getting ready for the rain," Dad said.

Dad had been checking the weather every night after calling Mom behind a closed door. We'd lie on the floor outside his room and listen as he begged her for a few more days.

When the storm came, Dad called in sick to work. With the first *tinks* of rain on the roof, he told us to hurry.

We followed him through woods that were thick with the smell of rain. The air had cooled. We reached out our hands and felt the trees' bark as we ran.

Dad stopped and pointed to the canopy of the woods.

"Sheets," he said.

We ran in circles beneath sheets that were hung between branches so high above us. Each sheet stained a different color. We outstretched our arms, our palms catching all different colors of rain. The strange rain dripped from our hair and down our faces. Reds and blues and purples. We opened our mouths and tasted it.

Some sheets were heavy with the weight of picked berries. Others colored with the dust of crushed creek pebbles.

When the rain lightened, our clothes were stained. Our tongues and teeth carnival-colored. We were laughing. Dad stood far away, watching silently.

The next morning we slipped back into the stained clothes we had begged him not to wash. And when Mom picked us up she shook her head.

"Couldn't even keep them clean," she said, before taking us away.

# Elephants

The day the river froze, The Pervert came to class with a black-and-white photo of a circus elephant hanging from a railroad crane. It was the day of our class presentations. LOCAL HISTORY: CLEECEY'S FERRY, TENNESSEE was written on the board in Miss Milligan's slanted writing. T-Boy nudged me when The Pervert pulled the photo from his backpack and put it on his desk. Two girls nicknamed the Prissy Sisters were giving a presentation about a woman who invented the windshield wiper. One of the sisters said that the wiper woman sold the idea to Cadillac. Said she used the money to buy a summer home in Cleecey's Ferry and never had to work again. The other sister wore a dress that looked like a picnic tablecloth and pretended to attach a wiper blade to a windshield made of cardboard.

When the girls sat down, The Pervert squirmed in his seat with his hand above his head. Miss Milligan looked for other volunteers. When no one else raised a hand, The Pervert walked to the front of the room holding the loose sheet of paper and had a smile wide on his face.

"There's an elephant buried in Cleecey's Ferry that weighs more than a school bus," The Pervert said. "At least before she died she weighed that much. Now she's just a skeleton in the ground by the railroad tracks."

T-Boy leaned forward with his elbows on his desk.

"And if you know where to look," The Pervert said, "you can see her tusks poking up out the dirt."

T-Boy looked over at me and made his arm into an elephant's trunk.

"Mary the Elephant preformed for the Sparks World Famous Circus until she went crazy and squashed her trainer's head beneath her foot like a spoiled tomato. The next day, the circus came to Cleecey's Ferry, but people refused to pay the price of admission until the crazed elephant was killed. They fed her apples as they led her to the tracks where she was hung."

As he talked, The Pervert passed around the picture of Mary hanging. A chain was wrapped around her neck and her feet were so close to the tracks it looked like if she could have pointed her toes they would have touched. I felt sick to my stomach. John Hackett made a trumpet sound, and one of the Prissy Sisters started crying as she held the picture of the dead thing. That brought Miss Milligan out of her seat. She snatched up the picture and pulled The Pervert out of the room by his elbow.

When the bell rang and Miss Milligan hadn't come back, T-Boy flicked my ear.

"Reece," he said. "We lucky dogs. I wasn't ready to get up there. Were you?"

I pressed my fingers against my pocket and felt the sixteen coins I'd brought to school.

"You think he's full of it?" I said.

"I know where she's buried," T-Boy said.

After school, I stood behind the baseball field and waited for T-Boy. I hadn't gone straight home after school since my mother got sick. I didn't like the smell of the house, or the way Dad tiptoed in and out of her room, telling me to be quiet and switching the TV off as he passed into the kitchen. T-Boy didn't go straight home either. On hot days we'd wade the creek, looking under rocks for things we could drop into the murky water of our Styrofoam cups. When the weather was bad, we'd spend saved-up quarters on the claw-catch game at the Dairy Queen.

I was scratching in the dirt with the toe of my boot and wondering about those elephant bones when I heard T-Boy's voice. It was the coldest day of the year, and nothing around had any color. Trees were gray-limbed silhouettes against grey sky. Yards were straw colored. Salt littered people's driveways and sidewalks, but there was no snow. It was too cold for snow. I shook the coins in my pocket to make sure they were still there. They were my grandfather's coins. I'd brought them in to tell the class how he'd found them at the bottom of the river beneath Benton's Bridge. In my pocket, they felt heavier than new coins somehow.

"Come on," T-Boy said.

We crossed through the woods behind school and followed the railroad tracks that led to Benton's Bridge.

"Think The Pervert got thrown out of school?"

"Don't call him that," T-Boy said, kicking some gravel at me.

"I heard that Coach Jennings walked in on him in the locker room. None of the showers were running, but The Pervert was butt-naked with two colored pencils up his ass."

"That ain't true."

"I bet you his shit looks like Skittles coming out."

T-Boy punched me in the shoulder.

"Keep it up," he said. "He told me if he got sent to the principal's office one more time his mom would send him off to reform school. Probably won't ever see him again."

"He told you that?"

T-Boy didn't respond.

"Is there really tusks coming up from the ground?" I said.

"Girl elephants ain't got tusks," T-Boy said. "Just like deer."

"Then how are we going to know where she's buried?" I said.

A few minutes later, we stopped at a concrete slab beside the tracks. It was covered in spray paint. There were dates written beneath initials and enough cuss words to fill a boy's head forever. Terrence love Stacey sprayed in blue. T-Boy stood on the slab and said we'd found her, that they'd paved her over after people started showing up with shovels, looking to take bones away as souvenirs.

I walked across the slab looking down at the black spraypaint outline of an elephant's trunk. Red paint, like blood, was leaking out the tip.

"They tried to shoot her first," he said.

"The Pervert's elephant?"

"I told you don't call him that."

T-Boy was looking up like he saw something in the trees. But I couldn't see nothing. I thought about bones hard as ice coming up out the ground. I thought if girl elephants did have tusks they'd be poking up into our feet.

The sky was thick with clouds that seemed not to move at all. Like they'd frozen there.

"Used a pistol," T-Boy said. "But it didn't bring her down. They had to hang her twice. The first chain wasn't enough. Snapped. And when she fell her hip bone broke so loud people could hear it when she landed. Like a tree splintering in a storm. And the ground shook because she was so heavy. People said they could feel it through the soles of their shoes."

"How you know all that?"

"I was at the library when he was looking it up."

"I didn't know you to go to the library."

T-Boy got quiet, and when he started talking again, it was almost a whisper. It was so cold I could see his voice.

"Sometimes," he said. "Lettie gets to yelling at Gary, then sees me and starts yelling at me for nothing. Gary will slip me a couple bucks and tell me to take off for awhile, until she cools down." Kids at school talked about how T-Boy's parents weren't his real parents. That his real parents were gone. Gary and Lettie took him in. I knew Gary was related to T-Boy some-way, but I never could figure how. T-Boy said they got a check every month that T-Boy lived with them, said they talked about it sometimes when they thought he was asleep.

"Never seen you read a book," I said.

"I just get on the computer. And they have sports magazines in the back. He's always there. Says he's not allowed to be at home alone. So he waits there for his mom to get off work."

T-Boy jumped off the grave site.

"Got something better to show you," he said, walking through the tall grass that grew beside the tracks. "Follow me."

"How you know the girls don't have tusks?" I said.

"My uncle took me out hunting a few years back, when he

was still coming around. He said we only shoot the males, the ones with antlers."

"I saw a ghost deer once," I said. "In the woods out behind our house."

"A ghost deer?" T-Boy said.

"Its fur was white," I said. "My dad says sometimes they're born that way. But it makes them easy to see, and so they don't live long."

"If it snowed, you wouldn't be able to see them at all," T-Boy said.

At school, the teachers told us the river had frozen for the first time in fifty years.

"Gary said his grandfather rode a bike across the river when he was a kid. Even all the way in the middle it didn't crack."

T-Boy spat on the train rails and bent down to see if it would turn to ice.

"How thick was it" I said.

"All the way thick," T-Boy said. "Frozen to the bottom."

"Rivers don't freeze all the way to the bottom."

"This one did."

"Bullshit. No river ever froze like that. There's always some water still moving beneath the surface."

I stood on the rail of the train track, balancing on one foot.

"Wonder how close the trains got to be for you to feel the rails shaking," I said.

T-Boy pushed me off balance and steadied himself in my place.

"So what were you going to give your talk about?" he said.

I took the coins from my pocket and told them where they'd come from, that my grandfather used to dive down and run his hands through the silt searching for wished-away coins, back when people thought prayers could be answered if thrown into moving water.

"My grandfather had to swim out there at night," I said. "He thought if people knew he was taking those coins they'd pull him out of the river and beat the snot out of him."

"And where did people throw them when the river froze?"

I fingered the coins in my pocket. Each was cold to the touch.

"I don't know," I said. "Never thought about that."

I felt my nose beginning to run, and the cold was pin-pricking the tips of my ears.

T-Boy snapped a twig from a fallen tree and held it between his two fingers like a cigarette. He blew out a mouthful of winter breath like it was smoke and started talking like he was in the movies.

"I'm gonna take off to California and change my name," he said between puffs.

I grabbed the collar of his jacket and tried to look serious.

"If you run, boy, you'll always be running," I said. "But if you stay." I tapped him in the center of the chest. "If you stay you can fight like a man."

T-Boy laughed and flicked his twig at me. I made a sizzle sound and pretended it burned my shoulder.

I'd seen my mother smoke a cigarette only once in my life, after her first doctor's appointment. I wasn't allowed to follow them inside. When she came out, she walked across the street to the filling station and bought a pack. Dad and I sat in the car while she stood outside and smoked. When she climbed into the car she looked back at me.

"First cigarette I've smoked in twelve years," she said.

When T-Boy and I got to Benton's Bridge, T-Boy threw a rock down at the river, too far for us to hear it hit the ice. The surface was dark with white cracks where the ice had splintered. I wondered if there were fish down there swimming up, trying to figure out what was above them.

T-Boy pulled at the sleeve of my jacket and pointed out at the center of the bridge. There were two brightly colored sheets hanging from the trestles like hammocks.

"What's that?" I said.

"I hung them there," T-Boy said. "Found them in the woods tied between the branches of a tree."

He turned away from me and headed out onto the bridge.

"Come on," he said, not turning back to see if I was following.

I could see the river through the gaps in the railroad ties, quiet and unmoving beneath us. I wonder what would happen if we fell, if we'd break through and drift downstream below the ice or if we'd land hard against it and hear the snap of our bones.

T-Boy slipped down between the rail ties and into the sheet hammock like he'd done it a million times.

"Don't worry," he said. "It's safe."

"Why's there two of them?" I asked.

T-Boy didn't respond.

There were candy wrappers in my hammock. I lowered one leg and tested my weight. The sheet tightened but didn't rip. I pulled at the knots to make sure they would hold. When I sat down, all I could see was the thick gray sky through the dark railroad ties above me.

"Reece, can I ask you something serious?"

T-Boy had never asked about my mom being sick, and I never teased him for having an uncle that showed up at school once without a shirt on and tried to steal the cafeteria refrigerator.

"Okay," I said.

"You ever felt a titty?" T-Boy said.

His voice came from the sheet next to mine. I knew he was smiling. When I moved, the fabric around me made a stretching sound.

"Mary Grace bent over my desk the other day," I said. "I could feel hers on my arm."

"I mean under the bra, stupid. With your hand."

I tried to think of something to say that wasn't a lie but not quite the truth either.

"No," I finally admitted.

"Me neither."

I was glad he hadn't.

"But he has," T-Boy said.

I imagined the Pervert in the backseat of his mom's car leaving Cleecey's Ferry forever, a crumpled black-and-white photo in his pocket.

"He went up a chick's shirt in the workout room at a Howard Johnson in Panama City."

I sat up in my hammock. T-Boy mimicked lifting a barbell with on hand and grabbing a breast with the other.

"I know which workout's better," he said.

I slapped his titty hand, and we both lay back and let our hammocks cocoon around us. We were laughing, but soon I remembered how high we were above the river and how something so thin was all that was between me and the ice below.

"These sheets are what I was going to give my presentation on," T-Boy said. "Gary showed them to me. There were these two brothers lived around. They heard about an underground spring that had water that could make sick people feel better. They figured they could make a lot of money if they found it."

T-Boy coughed, and I breathed into my hands to warm them.

"So they were out looking for it one day and saw this girl standing out in the woods. It was raining, and when they got close to her, they saw her eyelashes were so long she couldn't open her eyes. And they swore that the rain all around her was coming down in all different colors."

A train whistle sounded in the distance.

"Gary said she was the prettiest girl these two brothers ever saw. Sounds scary to me, but Gary said sometimes things can be both."

"So what happened?" I said.

"She disappeared. One of the brothers died in a train wreck in Nashville, and the other still hangs these sheets from the trees, paints them different colors so that when it rains it looks like the day he first saw her. Gary says he does it hoping she'll come back."

"Sounds like a story Gary made up to get you," I said.

T-Boy leaned out of his hammock and pushed against mine. We both started rocking, and I reached up and grabbed the ties above me to stop myself.

"Quit it," I said, worried the knots would come loose.

The train whistle grew louder, and T-Boy pulled my hammock close to his.

"Give me a coin," T-Boy said.

"They ain't mine."

"Just one so I can flatten it."

I handed him a wheat penny and he pulled himself up and set it atop the rail. I did the same and imagined it hot and flat after all those cars ran over it.

"Now grab on and let's see who can hold the longest."

As we both held onto that rail it began to snow. I knew that I could never hold longer than T-Boy. He had his tongue out collecting snowflakes. I felt the shake of the train. I let go and sat down. T-Boy held on until the train got so close it shook the coins from the track. If the world was silent, I imagined we would have heard two small sounds as they hit the ice at nearly the same time.

"Make a wish," T-Boy yelled, sitting back into his hammock.

I wondered how thick the ice would need to be to keep a coin from breaking through. I imagined two matching holes in the surface of the frozen river. Cold water seeping up and spreading a dark puddle over the ice.

The train came loud and shook everything around me. I closed my eyes and tightened my fists until I could feel my nails sharp against my palms.

When it passed, I heard T-Boy laughing. He was shaking his sheet to make it sway beneath the heavy rumbling tracks, like danger so close wasn't enough for him. I kept as still as I could. When the sound of the train was far off, I sat up and tried to see the coins but they were too small. I knew there was current down there somewhere. But all I could see was cold and ice and snow coming down heavy all around us. That noise still in my ear. That train so loud it shook loose the heaviest coins in the world. But not heavy enough to break through the stilled river. There was no dark puddle of water. The coins were quiet atop the hard surface, listening to the strong vibration of the current beneath them, and waiting for the ice to crack so they could find their way to the moving body of cold water, healing water.

T-Boy climbed up onto the tracks.

"What'd you wish?" he said.

"Can't tell you or it won't come true," I said.

I couldn't tell him I wished that elephant hadn't been killed, that there was no black-and-white photo of it that made me sick to my stomach. Because a wish like that was silly when there are moms that can't get out of their own beds and uncles that no longer come around and take their nephews hunting. And somewhere there's a boy getting sent to a school for kids who can't keep out of trouble. I didn't tell him I wished for something that couldn't be undone, something two pennies could never change.

"I wished to grab a titty beneath the bra," T-Boy said.

I laughed and knew he had wished for snow.

# *Jaima*

## SPOOK STORIES

Jaima let me sleep with the bathroom light on. She brought the phone into my room and put a cold washcloth on my head. Mom called from a truck stop payphone in some town I'd never heard of. Mom drove a big rig and made hauls all across the country. She said, Love you Junebug, goodnight. Love you sweet girl, goodnight. Then Dad called sometime later, sometime after I had fallen asleep. Jaima woke me up just barely and put the phone on the pillow by my head. Dad said, Sleep tight, don't let the bed bugs bite. I asked if he baptized anyone that day, and he told me he led an old man into a creek and had to dunk him twice because when the old man came up the first time he cussed the cold water, used the Lord's name in a way that wasn't quite Christian.

Jaima left the door cracked and hummed loud so that I could hear her from the other room. When I was scared at night, I liked to hear her voice. As long as she was singing, I knew nothing bad would happen. The doctor said I'd be back climbing trees by summer, but sometimes I had dreams where I never got out of bed. Jaima said little girls like me didn't need to worry about dying. Little girls just needed to think about skinned knees and skipping rocks well enough that they landed on the other bank without the tops getting wet.

In the morning, Jaima made pancakes with nuts and all of them were burnt on one side. She called the burnt side 'pancake bark' and we scraped it off with our fingernails, leaving dark flakes on the kitchen counter. Jaima said her mom never made pancakes, never made breakfast that she could remember.

The living room fan wobbled as it spun, and its chain moved in thin shadows across the carpet. Jaima stood on a barstool and spat her gum into the palm of her hand. She reached up and slowed the fan with her other hand and stuck the gum to the top side of a fan blade. I thought the blades would have hurt, but she smiled when they thunked against her fingers. I couldn't tell if the fan moved slower afterward, but that's what I imagined. That gum, still wet with her spit, slowing things just enough so that the world was different after she left, even just a little bit. But I think Jaima was just trying to make a sick girl smile and forget about how it hurt to stand up out of bed.

That night, I asked Jaima to tell me a spook story. It was two weeks after we brought her home with us to Cleecey's Ferry. I crawled into bed and asked Jaima to tell me the scary ones, the ones that really happened.

She told me that sometimes thunder is strong enough to shake a little girl's teeth loose from her mouth. Jaima lived next door to a girl in Mississippi who came home one night soaking wet with an empty mouth. The girl sleep-walked out into a storm, and the thunder cracked so close she spit her teeth into the tall grass. That's the world Jaima came from.

Jaima turned the light off and cracked the door so a thin tail of light stretched from the hallway into the dark room. She spoke in a whisper with a hand on the quilt covering my shins. I listened to her talk about the lightning and the thunder and a field scattered with lost teeth that the night animals carried off toward the darker places in the world only they know how to find.

When the story was over and Jaima was leaving my room, I asked her to hum until I fell asleep. I could hear the floorboards bending beneath her as she walked into the living room. She was humming something made-up, a song that never repeated itself.

I tapped the window above my bed and was glad for no storm. Not tonight. I wondered about them sleeping birds out there when all that weather starts up. Them clinging tight to twig nests. Cold rain and moments of electric blue that light up a sleeping world. How close does the thunder have to get before they come loose from the limb crooks where they are sleeping? How could the momma birds fly with feathers so heavy with storm water?

## DEER TICK

The doctor found a rash on the back of my thigh, and that night Mom ran an extension cord out to her rig and worked on the engine. She said we'd have bills that no amount of baptizing could cover, that she could go back out on the road like she did before I was born. I watched her work that engine until the whole thing shook alive. That was before Jaima came. Dad traveled most days baptizing people in divine water. Before I got sick, me and Mom drove around with him. I slept in the backseat, and Mom rode up front reading Dad his sermon notes and scribbling out the things that needed scribbled out. Jaima was a girl Dad baptized in the bay waters of Mississippi. When she heard I was sick, she moved to Tennessee and promised to watch after me when they were both on the road saving up money to make me better. Dad couldn't pay her much but she came anyway.

A few months after she came, Jaima started leaving the house in the afternoons and not coming back until after dinner. One night, I saw a car pull up, and Jaima snuck out the back door. When she came back a few hours later, she smelled like cigarettes and orange juice. She twisted her pinky around mine. I crossed my heart and hoped to die. I told her I could keep a secret, and from then on when that car pulled up, I'd pretend to be asleep when she came back into the house.

Jaima asked me if I'd ever kissed a boy, and I lied. Told her I kissed two boys that were twin brothers but didn't look alike. One had a loose tooth that he was scared to pull, and the other left his gum in my mouth. Jaima nodded like she believed me and told me I shouldn't be in a rush to round the bases.

I knew she wasn't talking about baseball, but all I could imagine was the first time I'd heard Dad cuss. In the summer, he liked to sit out on the back porch and listen to baseball games, and I knew sometimes they tried for a base they weren't fast enough for and got tagged out and everything was over. That's when he said, Horseshit as someone slid into third, and the umpire called him out, and the Braves lost a game they could never get back. He turned the volume down slowly when he saw I was watching him.

But it wasn't summer and dad wasn't on the porch listening to the game. I stared at things outside the window and wondered if I'd ever feel like getting out there again. Tree limbs low enough to climb swayed in the wind. Jaima carried me to the bathroom and sat me down. She waited outside with the door cracked until I told her I was ready. Sometimes I would finish and just sit until she knocked on the door and asked if everything was okay.

Dad hung a rope from the ceiling above the bathtub and told me never to let go of it when I took a bath. Jaima said he was worried because we didn't let him in there when they bathed me, thought someone would forget to keep an eye on me and I'd slip below, too weak to pull myself out. Sometimes Jaima and I could hear him in there, still wearing his shoes and standing in the tub, tugging at the rope to make sure it was strong enough to hold. Jaima would swing the door open quick just to scare him.

Jaima never asked what it was like, and I didn't know how to tell her. Dreaming of climbing a tree and falling into water so cold it took a few seconds to get your arms and legs moving, but in the dream they always got moving again. Only to wake up to the same bed you've been in for too long, knees and elbows aching. In a room where the only change was the way the shadows fell across the wall.

Are the spook stories in Tennessee the same as in Mississippi? And, Jaima, have you seen a ghost in this house?

She asked me how I would sleep if I knew snakes were shedding their skin in the walls of my room. Told me mice sometimes nursed their young in the folds of the couch and didn't even scream out when we sat down and crushed the babies. That there is a hemlock tree growing tall with bones wrapped in its roots. Some things cast shadows even at night, and some animals don't make noise when they walk. Jaima knew things kids weren't supposed to hear, and she'd tell me because some nights I didn't want to go to sleep. I'd stare at the ceiling and imagine every noise was some slithered thing wiggling out its own skin.

Some nights I'd start to cry, and Jaima would sit on the bed next to me. She'd say not to worry. That stories were just stories, and why do I ask her to tell me if I know they'll keep me up at night. I'd lay with my head on her thigh and she'd braid my hair. In the morning, I looked off balance, one side of my head thick with braids and the other side matted flat against my face from falling asleep in her lap.

## BAY WATER, MISSISSIPPI COAST

Jaima wore cut-off jean shorts when I first saw her. Mom said, Oh Lord, and fished a dress from her bag. Dad shook Jaima's hand, and she said, Pastor Glover, you baptized me a decade ago when I was about her age. Jamia pointed at me.

But I don't think the holy water stuck, she said. She said that if God had washed away her sin once, it was about time he make another go of it.

When she came out of the water, her thin dress was see-through and stuck against her body so you knew what every part of her was shaped like. I could even see the outline of a necklace against her chest, a metal feather hanging from the chain. Dad stayed waist deep in the water as Mom took Jaima away to dry off. She said Jaima needed privacy to get dressed, so she led her to the car parked behind St. Stanislaus School. Stanislaus, Dad kept saying, pronouncing it different each time. He picked up mussel shells from the beach, and we tried to skip them like rocks over the choppy bay water. None of them got very far. Mom and Jaima were gone a long time, and when they came back Jaima cussed under her breath after stepping on a piece of green sea glass. She told me, June don't you ever start. Foul mouth ain't something for a little girl.

Mom wrote our address on Jaima's forearm and after that we started receiving postcards once a week. When we told her I was sick, the post cards stopped coming. For three weeks we didn't hear from her, and then one day she knocked on the kitchen window.

When she was nervous she would flick her teeth with her finger nail, and when she slept her legs would jerk as she dreamed.

She kept found things in her pockets. Showed me acorns missing their caps. Creek gravel in the shape of shrunken faces.

The first night she was with us, she pinned autumn leaves to my window sill with safety pins she'd bent open and pressed into the wood. In the morning, the window was cracked just enough and the leaves shuddered as morning air came in, carrying with it the smell of dew. I wondered how she came into my room without waking me, and just then a strong wind caused all the leaves to ride up the safety pins as far as they could go. A half-dozen colored leaves hovering a few inches from the window sill, stirring against the whirl of the outside world.

## RAIN

Mom got home two days later than she was supposed to. For two days, Jaima didn't quit flicking at her teeth, and I got to where I couldn't stand to be in the same room with her. It was two months she'd been living with us. When Mom finally did come home, Jaima stayed sitting in the living room with the TV on like she didn't even hear the door shut.

Where you been, she finally said when Mom came in and cut the TV off.

Picked up another haul, Mom said.

Supposed to be back days ago, Jaima said.

We need the money, Mom said.

She came over to me and ran her hand through my hair.

How are you feeling? she said.

Jaima went outside to smoke a cigarette. She stood at the window and watched Mom and me. When Mom saw her, she crossed the room and fogged up the window pane with her breath. The ceiling fan made wobbling noises. Mom wrote something on the fogged window with her pinky finger, and when Jaima came back inside she was smiling.

That night, Mom carried me out to her truck and the three of us sat in the cab listening to the CB radio with all the lights off. Jaima laughed at the filthy things the men said and sometimes Mom turned the volume down and said, Easy now we got young ears here. Hanging from her rearview mirror was a Christmas ornament I'd made when I was younger. A popsicle picture frame and a green piece of construction paper with the words Merry X-Mas written in glue and sprinkled with glitter. Mom flicked the ornament, and the three of us watched it spin until the fishing line it dangled from grew tight and the spinning slowed. It lingered for just a second before beginning to spin again in the opposite direction.

Rain started up, and we watched it streak down the windshield. Jaima opened the passenger side door and said, Be right back. She came back soaking wet and holding an antique hand mirror and two wine bottles already uncorked. Mom put a pillow behind my head and kissed my hair.

Don't tell your father, she said, taking a bottle from Jaima. And if you get cold, honk the horn.

She shut the door, and they walked out into the rain.

Jaima lit a cigarette and hunched forward to keep it dry. Mom spun with her arms crossed, clutching the bottle of wine to her chest. Her face was up toward the clouds, and her eyes were closed. I wondered what the rain felt like against her eyelids.

I rolled down the window and listened to them laughing.

Jaima blew smoke at the mirror glass and announced she was watching the reflection of the rain.

Mom carried me inside, but I couldn't sleep. I imagined baby birds asleep in their nests, not knowing how to fly and worried that the thunder would get too close. The TV light gleamed beneath my door. I heard them talking. Then everything was quiet for a long time. I tiptoed across my room and cracked the door. Its hinges made a sound, but neither of them moved. They were asleep on the couch. Both curled and warm beneath the same blanket.

In the morning, our damp clothes lay in a pile by the back door. The mirror had a crack down the center, and when Dad walked in, he said it was like walking into a house lived in by strangers. The shower was running, and Jaima was in the kitchen making eggs.

We had a storm party, she said.

Storm party, Dad said.

Little one was tired of being inside, Jaima said, pointing a yolked spatula at me.

Mom came out of the bathroom wearing a white T-shirt and jeans. Her hair wrapped up in a thin yellow towel.

Home early, she said.

Dad sat down at the table and waited for breakfast.

I worry about them sleeping birds, I said, but no one seemed to hear.

## GLASS SAINTS

Dad was on the phone when Mom came through the back door. She had slept in her rig and was dressed in the same blue jeans and T-shirt from the day before. Jaima combed my hair, and we sat there listening to Dad mumble, Uh-huh, every couple seconds.

When he was preaching in some town far away and was gone for days, Mom would walk around in her sleeping clothes as long as she liked. Sometimes she stood next to Jaima making pancakes for dinner wearing one of Dad's T-shirts that came down to the back of her knees.

Mom said she had picked up a job when Dad hung up the phone.

Down through South Carolina, she said. Then off to Florida. Shouldn't be more than a few days.

Jaima pulled the brush through my hair and caught a knot. She yanked hard, but I didn't make a noise at the pain. Mom came over and kissed me between the eyes.

Take care of her, she said to Jaima.

Soon as we heard the sound of Mom's rig disappear, Dad said it was about time somebody clean the bathroom. He fished beneath the sink for supplies.

Jaima said she liked the smell of bleach and followed Dad into the bathroom. I could hear her talking, saying bleach made the air taste clean when she breathed it in. When he turned on the shower to wash the tub out, I couldn't hear them talking anymore.

A while later, Jaima came out of the bathroom and fixed a bowl of ice cream. She sat near me on the couch and asked if I was awake. I didn't open my eyes, and I tried hard as I could to breathe the way sleeping people breathe. When the shower went quiet, Jaima turned on the TV, clicked it to mute, and went out the back door. I waited a long time, knowing that when I opened my eyes I'd be alone in the room. When I sat up, Jaima was standing at the back door looking in at a TV she couldn't hear.

The kitchen sink dripped all night, and I couldn't sleep because the drips were uneven. Sometimes two came so close together it was hard to tell them apart, and sometimes I didn't hear anything for so long I thought there was no more water. But another drip always came, and I was worried the sink would fill and begin to leak onto the kitchen floor. I got up from the couch and stepped over Jaima who was sleeping on a pallet she'd made on the floor. I tiptoed to Dad's room and knocked lightly on the door.

Come in, he said. His bedside light was still on, and I could see that he had been crying.

What's wrong? I said.

Dad tried to smile.

It's never how you think it's going to be, he said.

He told me that when he was a boy he imagined the stained glass saints at St. Bartholomew's Episcopal Church could hear what he was thinking. They knew the sins he confessed when the congregation knelt in silence weren't the only sins he needed to repent for.

One winter, an ice storm hit and took down a tree beside the church. A limb crashed through the face of St. Peter. At church that Sunday, St. Peter's window was covered in plywood. The chapel was cold that morning, and when Dad knelt to confess, he saw a shimmer of red beneath the pew in front of him. He picked up the shard of stained glass and swore it burned his hand.

## MUTE

The last time Jaima snuck out of the house, she walked barefoot out into the night like she wasn't worried about stepping on things she couldn't see. Heat bugs seemed to grow louder when she was amongst them. I stood at the screen door and watched. Her footsteps were silent in the wet grass, and when she slammed the car door, it sounded like something breaking. Jaima stayed in that car long enough that I fell asleep for real, and when I woke up the car was gone, and Jaima was asleep on the couch with the TV on mute. A pill bottle and wad of dollar bills had fallen out of her pocket. There was a lady on TV selling knives that could cut through the sole of a tennis shoe, and I couldn't imagine ever needing anything that sharp.

## WEDNESDAY

The sky looked dangerous. The kind of weather Jaima liked to sit at the window and wait for. Dark clouds that hold on for as long as they can before they let go of everything, unleashing all that slanting rain. And that's how it was the day Jaima left for good.

She told me she needed to leave but couldn't until I was better. I started crying, and she hugged me tight. I could hear the drip of the kitchen sink.

Medicine's been working, I told her. It don't even hurt to stand anymore.

I got up and spun around to show her I wasn't sick anymore.

Jaima pulled me back onto the couch and put her cheek against mine.

Before you came, they'd yell most nights, I said. Before the sickness.

I don't know how long she held me like that. At some point, I was alone on the couch and wrapped in the quilt that smelled like Mom and Jaima all at the same time. And around my neck I felt the weight of Jaima's necklace.

I drew a picture of Jaima that night when I knew she wasn't coming back. But it didn't come out right. Dark hair not dark enough, eyes brown but not brown enough. And a smile that seemed not like her smile at all. Because I didn't have enough color to draw Jaima right. Jaima was something can't be captured. Jaima was once, and then Jaima was never again.

Jaima left on a Wednesday.

## FLECKS OF PAINT

Thursday night, me and Dad were the only ones in the house. Dad sat down on my bed and told me stories from the road. He was wearing the 1995 World Series shirt that he put on whenever there was painting needed done around the house. I listened to him talk and picked dried flecks of paint from his shirttail. He said you can't ever understand all of someone, can't know every part of them.

I wondered if Dad could smell her on the cushions the way I could. He leaned his head back like he was looking at the ceiling, and I brushed the paint flecks off his lap and onto the carpet. It was getting dark outside, but I left the lights off and waited at the window.

That car pulled up and parked, same as always. Headlights

off. Ember moving in and out the open window. If Jaima were there, she would have flicked her front teeth and said, Time for bed. She'd be smiling. Not smiling like she was happy, but like she was pretending to be. She'd come back in a while later and switch the TV to mute. That's what Jaima would do if she had been there. But Jaima wasn't.

I opened the front door without making a sound and walked barefoot through the dewing grass. A hand reached the burning ember out the open window and flicked it into the rain ditch. I heard the engine crank. When I got close, the tires made a screeching sound atop the asphalt, and the car was gone before I could see the face inside. When I turned back to the house, the front porch light was on, and Dad was standing behind the screen door. I raised a hand, and he raised a hand, and I think in that moment he was wondering what kind of daughter he was waving to, why I was out there alone in the dark.

I crossed back over the yard and didn't worry about stepping on things I couldn't see. My joints didn't hurt the way they had since the doctor found the rash on my leg. All those pills that caught in my throat when I tried to swallow were working. The ground felt good beneath my feet.

Inside, Dad rustled my hair with his knuckle.

Was I baptized? I said.

Dad locked the door and told me I was baptized in the church he and Mom were married in.

I don't remember it, I said.

He put a hand on the back of my neck. You were just a baby, he said, pulling me in.

I wrapped my arms around his waist.

She's not coming back, he said.

The ceiling fan muttered. The sink dripped. Flecks of dry paint littered the carpet.

I didn't know who he was talking about, but I knew he was right.

# Beneath Dark Water

**D**arcy hadn't said a word to Rae since she'd gotten home from the clinic. He listened to her repeat everything the doctor told her, about trimesters and prenatal vitamins. He didn't look at her as she spoke, and when she said she was sorry, he left the house, leaving the front door open.

There were three men with him when he came back. Men Rae had never met. Each of them carried a case of beer or a bottle of liquor. Rae assumed they were friends of his from before she'd met him, before he'd gotten clean. One of them set a plastic bag on the kitchen table. None of them spoke to her. Rae watched Darcy from the couch. He snorted a line of powder and drank Old Crow whiskey and chased it with warm 7UP.

It was almost morning when Rae decided she'd had enough. Through the window, she could see the sky beginning to lighten. She walked into the kitchen and took the bottle from Darcy's hand.

"Tell them to go," she said, not looking at the strangers standing mute around her. "And when they're gone, hook up the trailer." Rae emptied the bottle into the sink. She handed it back to Darcy and slammed the front door behind her as she went outside.

Darcy followed her. He had a beer in his hand, and she heard the crack of the metal tab as she climbed into the boat.

"We're going to take the boat out and run it 'til the tank's empty," she said, laying an orange life jacket over her knees and running her fingers over the broken plastic buckles. "You have to talk to me, Dar."

Darcy took off his ball cap, tilted his head back and put the cap over his face. Rae didn't say a word. Dawn was quick on the horizon. Darcy readjusted his hat onto his head and dusted some powder in the corner of his hand between his thumb and forefinger. He sniffed it and started to say something to Rae but walked to his truck and backed up to the hitch instead.


They were ten miles upriver when the engine quit. The boat settled into the water, its own wake washing around its sides. Darcy shook empty beer cans, looking for a few more swigs. Rae sat staring at her toes, hugging her knees tight to her chest. The current was calm and flat, but the dark sky promised bad weather.

It was a weekday morning, and there were no other boats on the river. No one to see him throw me overboard, Rae thought.

No one to see us if we make up and tangle ourselves in fishing line, lures dangling from our naked shoulders, hooks stuck in our bleeding skin.

"Gonna rain?" Rae asked.

"Always rains," Darcy said.

Darcy dropped the trolling motor and turned the boat so that they were pointing downstream.

"It's bullshit," Rae said, just barely a whisper. "Not like you've never run around on me."

"Not the same."

Rae watched a blue heron glide a few inches above the river. She wondered what it saw beneath the surface of the water.

"Not the same, my ass," she said.

Darcy pulled the trolling motor back onto the boat and sat down facing Rae. She figured he was studying the scar on her cheek, crooked beneath her right eye. The scar he sometimes touched when she pretended to be asleep. She wondered if he even remembered the girl's name who gave it to her. All she remembered was the sound it made in her skull when the lamp exploded against the side of her face. And how she'd bled into the carpet and wouldn't let him help her up. She could hear that girl gathering her clothes and running barefoot from the room as Darcy said *Rae, Rae* over and over again.

Hours passed. The boat drifted slow in the current. Darcy slept most of the morning and into the afternoon. Rae wondered why forgiveness came so easy to some people and didn't come at all to others. She paddled to the bank and tied the boat to a low-hanging limb. She looked at Darcy and then climbed out of the boat, unsure if they would ever make it home.

Rae walked through the woods that lined the river, collecting fallen buckeyes and thin peelings of cedar bark, things her mother had told her would bring good luck when she was a child. When she got back to the boat, she tossed a buckeye at Darcy. The sound of it ricocheting off the boat woke him.

"It doesn't have to be different than we planned, Dar," Rae said.

Darcy sat up but didn't meet her eyes. "All it's gonna be is different, Rae," he said. "Who knows what the hell that thing is even gonna look like."

"That thing?" Rae said. "That thing." Her voice was a slow wind beneath dark clouds.

The boat teetered when Darcy stood. He sat next to her and put his arms around her.

"Don't," Rae said.

He kissed her neck and kept his head on her shoulder.

"Just give me a name," he said. "I can handle this if you just give me a name."

Rae combed her fingers through his hair. Thunder echoed down the bluffs of the river.

"I told you I can't," Rae said. "I don't know what you'd do." She felt the muscles in his jaw tighten. "Hell, Dar, you don't even know what you'd do."

Darcy didn't speak. Rae pressed her hand against her belly, wanting to feel movement. She knew there was something growing in there she had wanted her entire life, something she would love. But all she felt was poison. Because what was inside her causing her to be sick in the mornings also changed the way Darcy looked at her.

The current took them toward the bank. Limbs submerged just beneath the surface scratched the bottom of the boat.

Darcy pointed at something floating in the water that looked like a twisted stick curling its way toward them. He grabbed a wooden paddle and raised it above his head. The paddle made a loud *crack* when Darcy brought it down against the water. The snake raised its head as if to get a better look at them. Rae saw its tongue tasting the air. She scooted to the far side of the boat. She'd always heard that cottonmouths nest their babies in the edgewater of rivers, just below the surface in the tangles of fallen trees or the hollows of old stumps. Rae's cousin told a story of a water-skier who lost the line and fell too close to the bank. Those on the boat heard him yelling that he'd fallen into a snarl of sunken barbed wire, that it was tearing the skin all over his body. When they pulled him on the boat, he was covered in baby snakes. And it's the babies you have to worry about. They bite quick and don't save any poison for later. Rae heard that boy was dead before they got the boat off the water.

"I've heard that too," Darcy said. "Told a hundred different ways by a hundred different people." He pushed off from the bank with the oar and let it drop back to the floor of the boat. They slowly drifted toward deeper water. "All bullshit. Cottonmouths don't nest like that. The babies take off on their own soon as they're born."

Rae scratched at her skin, thinking of how it must feel to sink into a bundle of baby snakes, their teeth sharp as razors. She hoped Darcy was right—told herself he was—and there wasn't anything to be afraid of. But she knew the kind of nightmares that waited for her when she fell asleep, knew it's the babies you have to worry about.

※

Before they knew each other's names, Darcy called Rae sweetheart when they were alone. He would come into the filling station twice a day just to see her. Dirty Braves cap and jeans stained with grease around the pockets. He'd pull a Coke from the bottom of the ice chest and wait until she wasn't checking anyone else out. He'd pay in exact change and say, *Thank you sweetheart*, as he turned to leave. Rae knew he probably talked to all the pretty girls that way, but she pretended it was just for her.

Then one day he didn't show up. She heard he'd been asking around about her. She figured he was working up the nerve to ask her on a date. For three days, Rae came in to work with perfume sprayed at her wrists and her makeup done. And for three days he didn't show. When he finally came in, he was wearing church pants and no hat. Rae could tell he'd tried to comb his hair. She wanted to tell him he cleaned up nice, but she was mad at him for making her wait, mad at the way people had snickered at her for wearing a nice dress behind a filling station counter.

He walked straight up to her without grabbing a Coke. "I'm Darcy," he said, reaching her his hand. "I was hoping you'd let me take you out."

"And when were you hoping to do that?" she asked.

"Friday night."

"I work Friday 'til eight."

"Well, I'll just park right out there on Friday," Darcy said. "Maybe when you get off, you'll feel like taking a ride with me."

He smiled and turned to leave.

"And maybe I won't," she called out after him, but he was already out the door.

Another customer was waiting to check out. Rae turned her back and tried to keep from smiling.

It was dark when Rae woke. She didn't know how long she'd been asleep. She'd been up all night, and they'd spent the better part of the day running upriver and floating back down, slow as driftwood. She rubbed her eyes. Her dreams had been tangled in the dark places beneath the water. Darcy was standing at the front of the boat, motionless. Rae sat up. She could smell fire. Above the trees downriver, she saw the glow of flames and the dense rising of thick smoke.

"What is that?"

"Don't know," Darcy said. "There's a bend in the river. Can't tell if it's on the shore or if the burning is coming from the water."

"Hope everyone's okay," Rae said. She could see Darcy clenching his fists in the moonlight. She thought about the muscles in his forearms tightening, the same forearms she had gripped onto so many times in bed. There was a strength in Darcy she was afraid of. Strength she had often hoped would keep her safe.

The smoke was a dark shadow against the blackened sky. Rae prayed for rain to come and put out whatever was burning so hot, prayed no one was close enough to the flames to feel the heat.

Before they came around the bend, she could see the reflection of fire in the current. Red glow flickering atop the water. Darcy picked up the paddle and started to row toward the blaze. The movement of the boat rippled the surface of the water and caused the reflected light to tremble.

"Don't," Rae said.

Darcy quit paddling and held the shaft with one hand, letting the blade trail behind the boat. When she saw the flames, Rae asked Darcy to sit.

"Barge fire," he said, and Rae scooted close to him.

The flames bellowed thirty feet into the sky. The air smelled of burning rubber. The fire roared an uncontrollable noise. She saw the light reflecting in Darcy's eyes. He wouldn't look away from the flames.

"Tell me something," Rae said.

Darcy talked toward the smoke.

"I ever tell you about my dad running the boat upriver to the lake?"

Rae didn't say she'd heard about it more times than she could remember. She wanted to hear something familiar.

"He knew every inch of that lake," Darcy said. "Where the fish were, what lure to throw at which log."

Rae could feel the warmth from the fire. They drifted toward it as if being pulled by the heat.

Darcy paddled the boat closer to the other bank.

"When I was little," he continued, "he'd hook one and keep it on the line until the fish wore itself out. Then he'd hand the rod to me. He'd tell everyone about it later, about the big fish I caught. I always felt guilty, everyone acting like they believed I'd really hooked it. And I remember once we went out there without any poles. He had him a cooler of beer and a couple Cokes in there for me. Only other thing he brought was this round magnet, looked like a weight at the end of a barbell. It was tied to a length of rope, had to be a hundred feet or more. Daddy just drank his beer while we ran upriver, and I sat wondering what in the hell we were doing."

They turned to keep their eyes on the fire. Rae rested her head against Darcy's chest and listened to the vibrations of his voice echoing through his body.

"When we got there, Daddy told me to keep an eye out for a dead tree taller than the rest. Said it was our guiding tree. He let me spot it even though he knew where it was. He got us right up next to the bank under that tree and turned the boat around, started heading out away from it. He was counting, looking back over his shoulder the whole time. One-Mississippi, Two-Mississippi."

Darcy counted the numbers out with his fingers as he talked. Rae waited until he got to five, took his hand and wove her fingers through his.

"When he'd counted off Twenty-Mississippi, he stopped trolling and dropped that magnet off the back of the boat. He'd given me gloves to wear, men's gloves that were loose over my hands. He told me to hold the rope, but not tight, just let it run through my fingers as the magnet sank to the bottom. When the line stopped running, he told me to pull it up."

Darcy dipped his free hand into the river and dragged his wet fingers over Rae's forearm.

"'We're on it,' Daddy said when the magnet came up with a rusty roof nail and a dinner spoon. So we dropped that magnet again and again. And again and again it came up with all sorts of metal. Silverware and door hinges, a letter opener shaped like a willow leaf, and a metal hairbrush with missing bristles. Daddy said when they dammed the river all sorts of people had to leave their homes. Some of them refused to go, stayed in their houses until the water came up through the floorboards. Neighbors had to come in boats and get them out, didn't even have time to pack up their stuff."

Rae imagined whole towns sunk beneath dark water. She saw

baby snakes slithering through keyholes, wrapping themselves around the handles of refrigerator doors.

"That water rose quick and took the roofs with it. Now there are all these houses at the bottom of the lake without roofs. And some of them still have dining room tables set for dinner, chests of drawers full of dead men's clothes."

The river turned, and the fire was behind them. All Rae could see was a faint glow of it reflecting off the rippled current.

"Before we left that day, Daddy threw the magnet in and brought up a pocketknife engraved with initials. The blades were corroded, but he gave it to me and promised he'd clean it up, get it sharp. But he never asked about it again, never polished it up. I couldn't even open it—the blades had rusted shut. I kept it in my pocket every day until I was old enough and had saved up money for my own boat. This boat. First time I took it out on the water I ran upriver to that lake. I found the dead tree and counted off Twenty-Mississippi. I stood there and drank beer and dropped that knife from the back of the boat."

"You never told me that last part," Rae said. "That you threw it back."

"Weren't my initials, Rae."

They stayed quiet for a long time. When Darcy finally spoke again, Rae had to lean forward to hear him.

"What'll it call me?" He sat slumped forward with his head in his hands.

"What do you want to be called?"

"I always imagined a mess of them," Darcy said, "running around, hiding behind my pant legs, calling me Daddy. And even last year when we saw that doctor and he said it wouldn't ever happen for me, I couldn't believe him. Still didn't this morning.

I looked at your belly and thought maybe it could be mine. But I see it in your eyes, you're so sure of it. You know it ain't."

"It can still be yours, Dar. You can still be Daddy."

"No. Can't be like that."

"It can be however we make it."

"Just like that? And we'll pretend forever?"

"No pretending." Rae knelt forward and rested her chin on top of Darcy's head. "No blood ever made a man a father. I got veins full of mine, and what'd he ever do for me?"

"Just tell me who, Rae."

Rae felt a quiet rain on her neck. She heard its small tinks sounding off the aluminum boat. Darcy didn't move, didn't flinch when the rain hit his skin or when the thunder cracked so close they could feel it. And he didn't look at her when she placed her hand against his cheek. Rae thought about the fire. She imagined the water beneath that barge warming from the flames. And about those baby snakes. She wondered if they would swim close enough to feel the heat, if they'd snap their jaws at the flames and crack their teeth trying to sink their poison into the metal hull.

Rae felt the coarse stubble on Darcy's face. She wanted to grab him in her arms and tell him everything would be all right. She wanted to dive into the dark water and see if the baby was too much weight for her. She wanted Darcy to watch her struggle to stay afloat and reach in and save her just as her last breath bubbled out from her lungs, to pluck her from the deep like something he'd keep in his pocket forever. She wanted to tell him the name she'd kept hidden so he could straighten everything back to normal.

"Tell me, Rae."

"Dar—"

"Tell me the goddamn name," Darcy shouted. He pulled her by the wrist, close enough that she felt his spit on her face when he spoke. "Tell me the name."

"No," she said.

Darcy swung quick and caught Rae on the side of the face before she could put a hand up to stop him. She had seen him punch men before. In a fight outside a baseball stadium in Chattanooga, and once in the parking lot of a Dairy Queen. And she knew this was different—this time he hadn't closed his fist. This time he'd kept his hand open and felt what it was he was hitting. Rae would have rather he punched her like she'd seen him do to those men. This was worse. This wasn't the bone of his knuckle, it was the palm of his hand. The hand she held when she woke up scared from nightmares, the hand that helped fasten her dress when she couldn't reach the zipper.

Rae sat down in the boat. Darcy watched her and chewed his lip. The rain was light but steady. The sky was still dark, but the thunder had stopped. Rae watched the wet drip from Darcy's hair down his face—the closest thing to tears she'd seen on his cheeks in a long time.

Rae dipped her hand into the water and left it there as the boat moved downstream. She moved her fingers, feeling for fish skin or snake tails. But all she found was the cold touch of water. She imagined that the river was depthless, eternal. A vein of dark current that had no bed.

Rae brought her fingers to her mouth and tasted the river. It made her think of a damp basement, the way rock beneath moss must taste. Rae reached into the water again.

"Ain't good for you," Darcy said. "Either of you."

"Since when does that worry you?"

"That water's dirty as hell. I wouldn't even swim in there."

Rae brought her fingers to her mouth. "Well I'm not you, am I?"

When they came up on the bank near their house, Darcy jumped ashore and pulled the boat up onto the grass. Rae stayed sitting. She could still feel the heat pulsing in her cheek where he had hit her, but she wasn't crying.

On the shore, Darcy unzipped his pants and relieved himself in the tall grass. Rae stood and stepped into the knee-high water, feeling the silt between her toes. She bent, took the river in her hand and brought it to her face. She knew if she were to see her own reflection, she would see that her blood had boiled to the surface, that his handprint was stained across her skin. She prayed the water would wash her clean, rinse away the pain that swelled on her cheek.

When she looked up, he was watching her.

"Hell you doing?" he asked.

She didn't respond.

"Rae, I'm sorry," he said.

Rae turned and waded into the river, pulling the boat back into the water. She felt the current pull at the hem of her dress. She waded deeper, until she could no longer touch the bottom.

"Rae, come back here," Darcy said. "I'm sorry,"

Rae climbed into the boat the way her mother taught her as a girl so it wouldn't flip.

"Rae," Darcy shouted. "Rae, where are you going?"

She rolled into the boat and fell onto the floor. She stayed that way, lying on her back looking at the sky. The current moved her downstream. She heard a splash and the rustling of water behind her. She knew Darcy was swimming toward the boat. She breathed deep and took in the damp smell of the stormy night. The clouds were thick and curtained the stars. She wanted to stare up at them until they broke, until something bright came through to lighten the night sky. Darcy was getting closer. Rae strained her eyes and asked God to thin the clouds and allow just one thing to flicker to life before she felt the boat tilt beneath Darcy's weight.

When Rae sat up, Darcy was close to the boat with his face in the water, swimming like there was something after him. She felt rain on her shoulders, rain that was growing heavy and beginning to unsettle the surface of the river. Rae bent and picked up the wooden oar. She gripped it tight in her hands and raised it above her head. *It ain't the babies you have to worry about* she thought. She brought the oar down hard against the water. It made a loud slapping sound that surely woke anything sleeping beneath the surface. Darcy stopped swimming and raised his head. He was close enough that she could hear his heavy breathing.

"Don't place one finger on this boat," she said. "I'm gonna float this river until the storm breaks. I'm gonna wait for the stars. If you're still back there when I see them, maybe I'll let you on."

Rae turned from Darcy and lay back down. She felt the cool rain soaking her hair, felt her shirt heavy and wet against her swollen stomach. She closed her eyes and waited. She knew that if she dove in now, she could stay above water forever. That she could kick her legs and swing her arms and keep breathing in the night air for both of them.

# *Seasons*

## AUTUMN

I didn't know you then, when afternoons were heavy with the smell of leaf smoke. Nights silent except for the heat bugs' screech and the coyotes barking at the coming rain. River barges moved slow with bright searchlights wary of shallow water. A single shoe hung from the bare limb of a dying tree.

A boy went missing and the divers found him in a lake near a park. You were at home watching the news alone. I was sitting at a bar reading the captions. The picture they showed of the boy, smiling with a blurry seesaw behind him, made you cry, but I wouldn't know that until later.

Did you know that there is a fire in the world that is older than Jesus? Where were you the night I stood alone at the water's edge and shaded my eyes from the barge's passing light?

I was working a job clearing trees from an abandoned stretch of land where the rundown house looked made of bark. There were splinters buried in my shoulders. The sound of heavy branches landing against branch-scattered ground. A man beside me lost an arm that was never found. They say you can feel things against the tips of your fingers long after the arm goes missing.

You lived in an apartment on Adams Street with puddles of candle wax caked against the hardwood floor. You let a man you called Jacob Number Two sleep in your bed on Sunday nights and sometimes called in sick to work Monday morning so you could pin his hands against the headboard. Details I asked you not to tell me months later but you did anyway and were confused when it made me angry.

The man with the missing arm's name was Elliot. A week before the accident, his wife brought him lunch on his birthday. She watched him eat it in silence and when she left she kissed him on the head and whispered *I love you* into his ear. He picks up his children now with the only arm he has left.

## WINTER

I asked your name at a party after we both had been abandoned. Jacob Number Two drank too much and fell asleep in a bedroom closet. My sister was on the roof smoking cigarettes. You lied and said your name was Always, but people called you Alwa for short. The lights were bright and someone had turned the music off. I touched your shoulder and you pinched the sleeve of my shirt and moved my hand. Be a good boy, you said.

Later, we kissed in the back of a taxi and when you got out you pressed your palm against the window and left a handprint. The driver drove too fast and I sat alone watching the tips of your fingers appear and disappear depending on the streetlights.

The second time I saw you, weeks later, standing alone outside of a restaurant. You climbed in the backseat of my car and pretended I was hired to drive you to a dinner party at the governor's mansion. You spoke in a British accent. Midnight and the field where you let your hair tangle in the dead grass. The tree strung with bedsheets like hammocks. When you fell and the broken finger. A hospital waiting room where you smiled when you found me still there. Blades of grass still in your hair. You slept on the couch until the lightning broke and you curled beside me. In the morning, you promised you were afraid of thunder. You held my hand with your bandaged finger, pretended you didn't see the bottle broken in the corner. Sweep up the shards. Bury them in the frozen ground. You asked if I believed in God and I put a fingertip against your eyelid after you fell asleep.

## SPRING

Mornings still cold, and nights we walked without shoes across the gravel. Black-and-white movies with the sound turned low. You read their lips instead and said things I prayed were meant for me. It only takes a forgotten look to break a heart. But we didn't know that then.

The staircase was swept clean. We listened to records before we fell asleep and I didn't drink after the sun went down. In the bedroom, we tied ribbons to the ceiling fan and left the windows open. Rain puddled on the hardwood floors. You kissed my neck and pretended to be in love. A bird died in the attic and when I came downstairs you were crying over another man.

Tell me I'll be okay, you said.

You are the prettiest thing in the world, I said.

That's not the same thing, you said.

You cut your hair short and drove two miles to scatter it in the river. You thought if we left it in the backyard the birds would make nests out of it and that it would stay in the trees a long time. I know now that you didn't want a part of you here forever.

## SUMMER

We walked through the woods with our shoes hung around our necks, the laces tied tight together. In the afternoon it rained. You went out into it and wet your hair. A child ran by pulling a wagon filled with acorns. Later, the pillowcase was damp. The shower fogged the mirror. You sitting on the toilet with the lid down lighting matches and dropping them into the sink. When I got out, you wrapped a towel around my waist. I took your hands and put your fingers to my lips. The scent of something burnt. You wiped a circle into the mirror and we looked at the reflection of ourselves.

You're kinder to me than I deserve, you said.

You deserve it, I said. I just worry I won't be around when you finally understand that.

We slept in bed with a lamp lit on the floor. I woke before morning. There was the sound of you sleeping. The sink piled with dirty dishes. I rinsed out a glass and filled it with warm water. You told me once that cold water ruins the metabolism. When I came back you were sitting up in bed.

I thought you had gone, you said.

Where would I go? I said.

Providence, you said.

Providence, I said.

Never mind, you said, I was dreaming about something I've forgotten.

The sun came up and you blew steam from your coffee into my ear. You were smiling. I thought it might have been the beginning of love but then you said, How do you expect this to work if we can't talk about anything?

What do you want to talk about? I said.

Nothing, you said and kissed my forehead, put your hand against my cheek. Your palm was warm.

Nights we swam against the wake of the quiet barges. Our toes lost in the river silt. And afterward, we dug up the broken glass and tried to walk across it without cutting our feet. The stars were faint behind distant clouds. Blood is unrecognizable against the shadows cast across the dew-wet grass.

## AUTUMN

A candle floated by one night, balanced on a length of driftwood. The bulb in the lamp by the bed burnt out. Where were you then?

## WINTER

A postcard from Rhode Island. A picture of a man standing on a boat with a cityscape in the background. No return address. A short note. "The state motto here is 'Hope.'"

## SPRING

The trees were empty of nests when the leaves began to bud.

## SUMMER

You were at the corner of our bar. The man next to you said-something that made you laugh. A baseball game was on TV. Bottom of the ninth. I left before you saw me. There was an accident on the highway that night. Paramedics loading a broken man into an ambulance. Police stood with hands in their pockets. Another man sitting cross-legged crying, his shoes balanced on the tailgate of a ruined truck. What was his name, the man sitting next to you at the bar? Do you remember?

## AUTUMN

I was living then in a motel by the interstate. A woman took phone calls for money in the room nextdoor. She told men her name was Faith. She smoked cigarettes outside when the phone didn't ring. One night the phone rang and she didn't answer. The fan above her ticked loud enough for me to hear it through the wall. The phone rang again. I closed the bathroom door. The tub was cold against my bare legs. I called you but you had changed your number. The woman in the next room emptied her ashtray into a storm drain and in the morning she was gone. I walked barefoot across the gravel parking lot.

## WINTER

I passed a store I had never been in and saw you inside. A car turned onto the street. The blink of its taillights. Your hair was longer. Two women were sitting on an upholstered bench watching you. One of them clapped her hands. You smiled and reached out to touch the lace sleeve of a white dress. People said it was warm for that time of the year.

# Shouting Down the Preacher

It was late morning. Hymnals soaked heavy with stormwater were scattered across the church, and the preacher remembered a day, years ago, when his wife left a window open and falling leaves fluttered in and settled among the empty pews. The floodwater had begun to recede but still covered most of the churchyard. The preacher's pant legs were rolled to the knee, his feet bare. A thin layer of silt hid the floorboards and he held onto the pew backs to keep from slipping.

The preacher carried stacks of hymnals and waded knee-deep toward the high ground of the cemetery. He folded them over gravestones to dry. A plague of cicadas pulsed in chorus from the tree limbs, their voices straining against heavy summer air.

Standing among the headstones, he watched a water snake

slither from the rain gutter of the church and across the shingles before it disappeared beyond the roof ridge. A mirror image of the church was cast across the surrounding water, only the slow ripples betraying what was reflected from what was real.

When the hymnals were all moved, the preacher sat on the front steps of the church and picked mud from beneath his toenail.

"Won't be the last," he said. It was what his father had always said after a storm had passed.

It had been three years since he lost his congregation. In the supply closet, he found a box of stale communion wafers untouched by the flood. He tossed them one by one into the still water. Fish broke the surface, taking the wafers whole and churning the water as they disappeared.

"Body of the Lord," the preacher said.

All around him the scent of unsettled mud and murky water. A smell that reminded him of baptism.

The preacher was forty-one years old and, depending on the time of the year, was often mistaken for a man much younger than he actually was. He had lived alone for 1116 days and kept a yellow legal pad on his bathroom sink where he recorded the diameter of a mole on his left shoulder blade. It was something his wife had suggested, something that he hadn't done until the morning he found their medicine cabinet empty of her things.

A sound came from behind the church. Like stones being dropped into shallow water. The preacher listened but kept his eyes fixed on the cemetery.

The hymnals folded over the gravestones looked like strange birds perched silent and waiting. The sound came again, and the preacher stepped off the porch and waded around the side of the church.

A boy stood with one hand touching the high-water mark staining the wall. His shoes hung around his neck, the laces tied together.

"Jarfly," the boy said when he saw the preacher. He picked the shell of a cicada from the weathered clapboard siding just above where the water had settled.

"My daddy called them screech bugs," the preacher said.

The boy cupped the insect husk in his palm. He had taken off his shirt and tucked it into the back of his pants. Damp leaves were stuck against the tan skin of his chest.

"There is a drowned man tangled in a tree," the boy said, pointing toward the river.

The preacher could make out where the bank should have been by the line of trees that grew out of the current. Their trunks lost beneath the risen water. The preacher trudged behind the boy, struggling to keep up.

Other children's voices came in whispers behind half-sunken bushes. Flickers of movement and the splash of bare feet.

"There," the boy with the jarfly said, pointing at a dead tree in front of them.

A pair of mechanics' coveralls had been caught in the branches. The legs dangled and trembled in the breeze. The arms were twisted in the limbs and the preacher could see a name stitched across the breast but couldn't make out the letters.

"It's only clothing," the preacher said. "Washed downstream with the storm."

The boy with the jarfly put a finger to his lips then pointed at a pale child with ash in his hair climbing a submerged tree trunk just below the surface of the water. The pale child stood, seeming to balance on nothing but water itself. He picked buckeyes from an eddy around his feet and spat on them before he threw them at the dead man.

"Knock him from the limbs," the pale child said.

Other children emerged from their hiding spots and swung sticks of bamboo at the dead man's legs.

"Fall mister dead man. Fall."

The preacher withdrew. Back toward the church and up the stairs. Inside, he was careful not to slip on the slick floorboards. He watched the children through the opaque glass of a window he'd once kept clean. He used to stand at the same window while his wife played tag with Sunday School children. She knew the kind of magic that could calm a skinned-kneed child from tears. She could weave a four-leaf clover into a braid of hair so tight that all the cartwheels in the world couldn't shake it loose.

The preacher took his phone from his pocket and dialed her number from memory. He hadn't had a cell phone before she left. She used to take photos of him with hers and tease him for the surprised look that always seemed to be on his face. Sometimes, he wondered if she deleted those photos after she left. Or if maybe, she looked at them now and then and imagined herself smiling.

When she moved out, he bought a prepaid phone with three hundred minutes programmed into it. He kept it in the glove box of his car and the first call he made was to a radio station contest offering a gift certificate to the restaurant his wife worked at when they first met. The preacher called in and named all three presidents that died in Tennessee and what years they were in office. The DJ told him he'd won, but the preacher hung up the phone instead and put it back in the glove box.

"I need your help," the preacher said when his wife answered.

"William?" she said. "Where are you?"

"At the church," he said.

"At the church?"

"There are children here," the preacher said.

"What children?"

"Something from the storm got caught up a tree," he said. "They're playing like it's someone drowned, someone washed away."

"Okay," she said. "I'll be over soon as I find my shoes."

"Don't wear any can't get ruined," he said, but her end of the line was already dead.

Half an hour later, the preacher's wife pulled up to the church and parked at the far end of the gravel lot that was above water. She walked past the open doors of the church without looking inside. The children turned toward her when she was close enough that they could hear the splash of her feet. They dropped the things they were holding. She had taught them Bible stories on Sunday mornings and Wednesday nights. They knew her as the woman who would wrap a lost tooth into a Kleenex and put it gently into a coat pocket.

The preacher stood at the window as his wife led the children away from the tree where the drowned man was tangled. Her hair had grown long, and he wondered if it still smelled like rain. She used to stand naked beneath the eaves of the house and bathe in storm water. The preacher would watch her from the garden shed where he wrote his sermons. And it was those sermons, written while his wife stood naked and lightning cracked and thunder roared, that always brought his congregation closest to God. Praise Jesus, they shouted, their palms raised toward the ceiling. And when he called them to confession he'd watch them unfold the kneelers and bow, silent lips mouthing their sins. He'd whisper to God and ask to be forgiven for the rain. Because it was the rain that he prayed for at night.

The preacher lifted the window and listened to his wife talk to the children. She touched each of them on the back of the neck and told them drowned man was sleeping. She told them he'd climbed the tree to see a robin's egg crack, to see new wings shiver for the first time. She taught them how to pucker their lips and call out a bobwhite whistle.

The children ran toward the cemetery whistling. The preacher's wife followed and picked a hymnal from a gravestone. She hummed a melody the preacher recognized. A girl with thick glasses stood and unfolded another hymnal from a gravestone and began to sing. As she sang, the screech bugs grew quiet in the trees. When the child finished her verse, the boy holding the jarfly stood and started a new song.

And then another child. One by one the children unfolded the hymnals and joined the choir. Each singing a different verse from a different damp page, but to the preacher it sounded like something almost familiar. Like a dream of something once forgotten.

"Are you listening?" the preacher said aloud in the empty room.

It was dusk. The preacher stepped out of the church. He crossed the flooded yard and climbed the tree where the drowned man hung. He imagined crimes scenes from the TV shows he watched late at night. In the branches by the mechanics' coveralls was a fishing lure, the hook stuck into the bark of the tree. The preacher untangled the coveralls and read the name stitched into the breast before dropping them into the water below. Grayson was the drowned man's name. The preacher pulled the fishing lure free and scraped the name into the tree bark with the sharp point of the hook before climbing down and walking to the cemetery.

"Thank you," he said. It was the first thing he had said to his wife in three years. "I didn't know who else to call. Seemed dangerous, them playing out there so close to where the riverbank drops off."

The preacher's wife nodded and smiled a tight lipped smile.

"Never did know how to handle kids," she said.

"They always scared me somehow."

"You would have learned," the preacher's wife said. She looked back over her shoulder at the children running among the funeral stones and then took the preacher by the arm and waded toward the church.

"Everything ruined?" she said.

"Piano's fine," he said. "Water didn't quite make it up to the keys."

"So the communion cabinet?"

"High and dry."

"Well," she said. "He brings the water, we take the wine."

The preacher's wife entered the church and returned with two unopened bottles.

"It's getting dark," she said. "We ought to get these kids home."

All the children climbed into the bed of her pickup, except the boy holding the jarfly.

"I can walk," he said.

The preacher ruffled the boy's hair.

"He can walk," he said. "Doesn't live far."

The boy disappeared around the back of the church, and the preacher followed his wife to her truck.

"Climb in," she said holding up a bottle. "Let's go ride out the evening."

It was something they used to do every Sunday, after the sermon was given and the church emptied. She would drive and he would stare out the window at the country passing by. They'd both sip from the bottle. Sometimes, if he saw an abandoned house or rundown building, they'd pull off to the side of the road. She collected antique door knobs, said the smooth feel of the porcelain was something that reminded her of the house she grew up in.

The children in the bed of the truck were calling out the names of nighttime animals and doing their best to imitate rain owls and tree frogs. His wife was humming a lullaby he'd never heard before. She had never complained that they had not had children of their own, but he had often noticed her counting the children playing in the churchyard, pointing to each one and mouthing a number, making sure none were missing.

The preacher's wife took her foot off the gas and slowed the truck without touching the brake. Her eyes were fixed on the rearview mirror. The preacher turned and saw the pale boy standing, twirling a pair of red-laced shoes he had taken from around the neck of a smaller child. When the smaller child reached for the shoes, the pale boy threw them above his head and the white shoes dangled there against the darkening sky. The preacher waited for them to fall, but they never did.

"Telephone wire," his wife said, smiling.


The last child patted the tailgate and ran down a short dirt driveway. Lights were on inside the house and the preacher could see a man standing over a stove, spatula working something in the skillet.

"Like old times?" the preacher's wife said, pulling a corkscrew from the glove box and opening a bottle.

They drove in silence, each taking slow sips. She rolled the windows down, and the night air was warm and damp against their faces.

When she spoke, it was such a small noise he thought he might have imagined it.

"I need to know how it happened," she said, dimming the headlights as a car passed going the opposite direction.

"You told me you didn't want to hear it," the preacher said. "Not one detail. Close the door, board it up."

"That was a long time ago."

The preacher turned the radio volume low and rolled up his window.

"Okay," he said.

"Who was she?"

His wife left her window down and kept her hand out in the breeze, as if touching something familiar.

"Told me her name was Loralee," the preacher said. "She was in town for the summer. Staying with Jim and Betsy Carol. Their niece, I think."

The preacher's wife steadied the steering wheel with her knee and took a long drink of wine.

"It only happened the once," he said.

"Keep going," his wife said.

"She came in late on Thursday night, after prayer meeting. Your sister was sick and you went to Knoxville to help with the kids."

"I remember," his wife said, flicking the high beams on.

"She came and asked if she could confess. I told her it wasn't that kind of church, but she went at it anyway. Told me she'd been swimming naked down beneath Sycamore Falls. That she went every night around sundown."

"How old?"

The preacher looked at his wife for the first time since they'd started talking. Her lips were wine-stained. He remembered the first night they had slept together. How he woke up in the morning and she was gone, still working breakfast shifts at the restaurant. When he got up to get dressed, he noticed himself in the mirror, a red lipstick kiss on the center of his forehead that hadn't been there the night before.

"Twenty maybe," the preacher said. "On summer break from college."

"Skinny dipping isn't much of a sin," his wife said.

"And I told her that," he said. "It was what went through her head standing in the falling water that worried her."

The preacher stopped and twisted the corkscrew into the second bottle of wine.

"Are you sure you want to hear this?" he said.

His wife took the bottle from him and drank.

"I'm a big girl," she said and handed it back to him.

"She would dive in and hold her breath long as she could and hope someone, some stranger, was watching her when she came up. Said she imagined doing things with that stranger she couldn't say inside of a church building. And then she stood up from the pew and left."

"And you followed her?"

"No," the preacher said. "The next day, I drove past the

trailhead that leads to Sycamore Falls two or three times. Even parked once. But never stepped foot on the trail. I didn't. It was getting close to dark and I drove back to the church and sat in the last pew and went over my sermon."

The preacher's wife slowed the truck to a stop. There was a gaze of raccoons crossing the road. The mother straddled the center line until the last of her cubs had crossed. Her head was cocked, looking into the headlights, eyes reflecting back bright and still.

When the road was clear the preacher's wife took her foot off the brake.

"She knocked on the open door of the church while I was sitting there," the preacher said. "She was dressed, but her hair was dripping. It made a puddle on the floor when she stepped inside."

"Jesus, William," his wife said. "In the church?"

"She said she had waited for me," the preacher said. "That it got cold when the sun went down. I grabbed a towel from the baptismal closet and led her outside."

"Where'd you take her?"

"She told me she was leaving the next morning, back to school. Community college somewhere, I think."

"Where'd you take her?"

"That picnic table by the boat ramp," the preacher said. "The one you won't eat at."

"Where we got stung by hornets," his wife said. "Had to jump in the river to get away from them."

The preacher leaned forward and put his head against the dashboard.

"You never told anyone why you left," he said.

"No," his wife said.

"Why?"

"I thought the congregation needed an example to follow, even if it wasn't real."

"Well, that example didn't last long," he said, and for the first time that day the preacher's wife laughed.

"Oh, I heard," his wife said. "Everyone talking about you losing the spirit."

"You can't even imagine."

"That bad?"

"I couldn't keep focused a minute. Would lose my place and forget whole passages of scripture. Every week the pews grew emptier. At the end, I was up there talking about Jonah. Started breaking down the intricacies of life inside a living animal. How a whale passes gas two hundred times a day, that there is enough of it inside to allow a human to breath for hours."

The preacher and his wife looked at each other, both smiling.

"Honestly," the preacher said. "I don't know what the hell I came out my mouth."

"Quite the sermon to go out on."

"Wasn't the last," the preacher said. "Tried again the next week. Didn't get a minute in before Terry Beals stood up, both hands to the ceiling. 'Jesus,' he shouts. 'Holy Jesus. Give this man back your tongue.' I tried to speak louder, to follow my sermon notes, but Terry kept screaming. And then Benton Cray starts at it, asking God to return His spirit to my soul. Soon enough the whole place is shouting, so loud I just folded up my notes and sat down behind the pulpit."

"Shouting down the preacher," his wife said.

"That's how it ended," he said.

When they pulled back into the gravel parking lot, the doors of the church were swung wide and they could hear piano notes being played at random from inside. The preacher's wife left the engine running and filled a paper cup with wine.

"I used to love playing that piano in the dark," she said.

The preacher remembered following behind her on warm nights when she would walk barefoot to the church. It was a game they played. She'd sneak out of the house after they'd made love on the screened-in porch. When he noticed she was gone, he'd trail her to the church and sit quietly as she played. Soon as the music stopped and he heard the thud of the fallboard, he would jog back to the house, and they would both pretend that she had never left.

"You didn't have to stop," the preacher said. "You know where the spare key is hid."

"Wouldn't be the same," she said.

The notes from inside the church stopped and the boy holding the jarfly came outside. He shielded his eyes from the headlights and walked to the driver's side of the truck.

"You want a ride?" the preacher's wife said.

"I never played a piano before," the boy said.

The preacher's wife opened the door and stepped out.

"Come with me," she said, leading the boy away from the dry gravel parking lot and back through the floodwater.

The preacher followed but didn't go inside. He sat on the porch watching the reflection of the moon reaching out over the flooded churchyard. The preacher listened to his wife's voice as she explained the names of the keys and the difference between the white and the black ones.

The preacher stood when she began tapping notes and walked around the side of the church. He balanced one-footed atop a water spigot coming out the side of the building and looked in through a window. His wife placed the boy's fingers over hers so that he could feel how the right notes were played. The boy set the jarfly where the sheet music should have been and the delicate insect shell shook with every note. The hymn was "Just As I Am," and the preacher mouthed the words as best he could remember.

His wife used to sing along to songs she didn't know as they came on the car radio, a half-drunk bottle of Sunday wine between them. She'd sing her own made up songs with the volume turned low. Her lyrics were always strange and beautiful, stories about worlds where storm clouds could freeze and the only color that existed was the color of the sea.

When the song ended, the preacher walked back to the front steps and sat. A coyote yelped from a nearby hill and the preacher wondered what it must be thinking looking down at the only world it ever knew turned to water. Tiptoed steps sounded on the floorboards behind him. When he turned, he saw the boy standing, the jarfly missing from his hand.

"Was that you playing in there?" the preacher asked. "I'd say you're a quick learner."

The boy smiled.

"She said I could come back," he said. "That she'd teach me."

"She tried to teach me once," the preacher said. A firefly made ripples in the water near the porch, beating its wings to try and take flight. The preacher picked it up and watched it crawl across his fingers and flicker once before it flew away. "But I wasn't a natural like you."

The boy walked barefooted through the water and then across the gravel parking lot without slowing his pace.

It was quiet for a long time before the preacher's wife began playing again.

The floodwater would recede after a few days and the land would become normal again, but while his wife played the piano, the preacher waded out and was thankful. When the song ended, he hoped that she would play another, hoped the river would rise and lift the church from its foundation, that the current would take the whole building downriver, and as it drifted away his wife would play song after song. He would float on his back following behind, listening.

The fallboard made a dull thump and footsteps creaked the floorboards. His wife stopped in the entrance of the church and leaned against the doorjamb.

"Need a lift?" she said.

"I can walk it," the preacher said. "Figure I'll stay a while longer."

He stepped up onto the porch closer to her.

"Don't want another?" he said, offering her the rest of the wine.

She smiled at him. Above them, critters scurried across the attic floor.

"Figure I should get some poison tomorrow," he said. "I imagine all sorts of things crawled up there to flee the storm."

"They die up there, they'll start to smell," the preacher's wife said. "I've got some traps, won't kill them."

"I'd appreciate it."

"I'll bring them by tomorrow," she said. "If the doors are open."

"I'll be here," the preacher said.

"I think that's a good thing," she said. "Sad thing seeing a church locked up seven days a week."

The preacher's wife pinched her dress and pulled it high,

keeping the hem from dragging atop the water as she walked to her truck. She was humming, and the preacher listened until she cranked her engine and pulled away.

When her headlights disappeared around a bend in the road, the preacher stepped back inside the church. Critters scratched across the ceiling. The room smelled of mildew. In a storage closet, the preacher found a camping lantern and set it on the piano. He ran his fingers across the fallboard, felt dust on his fingertips. Her cup of wine was half-full on the seat next to him. He brought it to his lips.

"Blood of Christ," he said. "Given to you."

The jarfly was resting there against the music rack. The preacher blew at it and the paper thin skeleton quivered. During the worst of the plague years there would be billions of them. The preacher remembered a Sunday they were so loud he had to end his sermon halfway through because he couldn't shout over their noise.

At the piano, the preacher blew and blew, waiting for the jarfly to come apart and crumble. He lifted the fallboard and pounded the keys, the deep notes, harder and harder. The dead thing trembled but didn't break. When the preacher stopped, there was sweat running down his cheek. He wiped a sleeve across his forehead as he stood and picked up the camping lantern. The night bugs were quiet in the trees around the church.

The preacher walked to the front and closed the doors. He turned the lantern off and sat down on the last pew. A stillness took hold, only broken by the sound of his breath. The preacher closed his eyes.

When he woke, it was to the sound of a soft whine. The preacher opened his eyes, but all he saw was moonlight and shadow. Then the noise came again, stronger. And again. A screech growing so loud the preacher worried it would splinter the windows.

He stood and stepped toward the front of the church, toward the screeching. He stopped halfway down the aisle. The whisper of dry paper wings fighting to grab hold of the thick night air, a whisper that turned into a buzz and a whirl of something taking flight.

The preacher turned and rushed to the church doors. He flung them wide. Fireflies blinked back at him from the tree line and something quick hummed by his ear, close enough he could feel the air being disturbed as it passed.

The jarfly landed on the railing of the stairs close enough that the preacher could have touched it. Beyond, the moon's long reflection fluttered as a slow breeze rippled the floodwater. The jarfly let out a long, high screech. And from all around the church, the night insects echoed in response. All of them, shrill voices, turning the still night into something vibrant.

The jarfly took flight and was lost into the heavy pulsing of a night come alive.

It had been three years since the preacher stood alone on the porch of his church and prayed, and when he closed his eyes he didn't know how to begin. So instead of a prayer, he listened to the cicadas, the jarflies, the screech bugs, and for a moment the floodwater began to rise and he could feel the church breaking free from its foundation.

When the preacher opened his eyes, he said, Amen.

# How to Hang a
# Circus Elephant

**SPARKS WORLD FAMOUS CIRCUS SHOW.
SEPTEMBER 1916. TENNESSEE.**

Buy your tickets early. Fold grocery sacks into crown hats for
the children and decorate them with crayon drawings of lions
standing on two feet, trapeze artists reaching for waiting hands.
Let the children wear their crowns to school. Remake them
when it rains.

Wake up late in the night and assure the youngest that the
scary animals aren't dangerous, that their teeth are rubber.
Their claws dull and round. Sit at the foot of her bed until she
falls asleep. Wake your wife and ask if the scary animals are
something you should be worried about.

In the morning, go out for the paper. Read the story of a crazed animal that killed her trainer forty miles away. Mary the Elephant, eight thousand pounds, stepped on her trainer's head and flattened it like it was spoiled fruit. The next stop in the circus tour is your town.

Burn the paper in a rain ditch before walking home. Your children are sleeping.

The circus crowns are folded on the table. The stove is steaming a pot of warm water.

Your youngest comes into the kitchen first rubbing sleep from her eyes. She fits her crown in place and rests her royal head on the table.

This is the day you'll be asked to hang an elephant.

Before breakfast is over, listen to the neighbors outside planning. A boycott is called for. Refunds demanded if the killer elephant isn't put down. Teenage boys throw handfuls of roofing nails at the circus cars. A street preacher announces the beast is inhabited by a demon named Belial.

Leave the children at home. The circus master is talking to a crowd of swarming people. Mary the Elephant is in a pin behind him, eating sweet potatoes from a pile in the dust.

A local man whose face you recognize produces a pistol. The circus master hands the pistol to a carnival employee, who checks to see if it is loaded. The circus master isn't seen again that day. The circus employee climbs a tree above Mary's pin and fires three shots into the back of the animal's head and neck.

A pistol is not strong enough to kill some elephants. Mary moans and rears up on her hind legs, but when she comes back down she is still standing. She blinks. Blood drips from her eye and from the side of her mouth.

A discussion is had, a decision made.

Mary the Elephant will be hung by the neck from a railroad crane.

This is when you hear your name being called. A strong hand grips you by the elbow.

You are the local station agent for the railroad. You will unlock the train shed where the crane is stored.

When you hang an elephant, it is best to tighten three chains around its neck, but you won't know this yet.

On this day, you fix one chain to the animal and begin to lift her above the tracks. A crowd has gathered. Men, woman, and children all cheer and applaud. Kill the beast! Hang Miss Mary, hang!

The first chain breaks and Mary falls. The sound of her hip snapping silences the eager crowd. The weight of the animal shakes the ground, and for years people who were there will talk about the shudder they felt through the soles of their shoes. A young boy begins to cry. Mothers lead stray children home.

Call for heavier chains. When you lift Mary from the track this time there is no applause. Her feet hang less than an inch from the rails and if she were only able to stretch her toes she would feel the smooth metal tracks.

Bury the animal in a patch of dead grass beside the railroad. Weeks later you'll have to dig her up and rebury her in an undisclosed location, because school children were digging for souvenir bones.

In the days after her death, little else is talked about. Tell your children Mary was sick. Mary is with God now, knee deep in cool water blowing a trunkful high into the air.

The trainer that was killed had been hired the morning of his death and had no experience with animals big or small. He used a bathroom mop sharpened to a point to prod her from her cage. Just before she trampled him, he jabbed her in the left cheek as she was attempting to chew on a watermelon rind.

An autopsy after her death found a large abscess inside Mary's mouth on her left jaw, an abscess that, if known about, should not have been irritated.

On this day, after the silent crowd dissipates and the crane is locked in the dark train shed, return home. Fold the paper crowns and hide them beneath the thick attic insulation where, hopefully, the children won't think to find them.

# Dryland

I t was fall of 1995, the Braves in Atlanta were making a run
at the pennant, and all I knew about love was that my father
was following my mother to Florida to try and sort it out.
I was lying flat on my stomach in my grandfather's makeshift
attic, plywood laid across the exposed beams of his bedroom,
listening to voices he kept hidden in a shoebox at the bottom of
a wicker trunk filled with patchwork quilts. I had a wish penny
in each of my pockets. I was nine years old.

The voices were recorded onto cassette tapes labeled with
street addresses that belonged to houses forgotten at the bottom
of the lake. They spoke of the slow construction of the dam. Of
things they'd lost when the water rose. One sang a song.

Thursday morning, the day of the week the piano tuner came.

My grandfather's bedroom was empty of furniture except for the canopy bed and the grand piano, a hand drawn map spread across the floor. On the wall there were bird feathers framed behind glass and hung at different heights. Dozens of them. Blue feathers, small and thin as pinky fingers. A long raven's, like spilt ink. Rain owls. White egrets. The frames he had made himself from driftwood he collected from the shore in the mornings before the sun was above the timbered horizon. In the garage he carved them. Wood glue and pin nails. Thin glass cut to size. At night, before he turned his lamp off, I could sometimes hear him imitating the calls of the birds whose feathers surrounded him. The bobwhite, the screech owl.

The piano tuner found a peacock's plume feather on the hood of her car one afternoon. It was blue and green but its color seemed to change depending on the angle. My grandfather strung it with fishing line and hung it from his ceiling fan.

A woman on the cassette tape spoke about a coin purse filled with marbles hidden beneath a porch board, how she'd forgotten it until the car was packed and pulling out onto the highway. The woman was a young girl then and remembered crying for hours after her father refused to turn around.

When the piano tuner came in the room, I turned the volume low and stayed still and quiet. She set her leather-wrapped tools on the bed and let down her hair. It was long and dark like my mother's and I wondered if it smelled the same, like rain water caught in a cupped hand.

I'd been sent to my grandfather's house the night my mother came to the dinner table wearing a pair of earrings my father had bought for another woman.

"Do I look pretty to you now?" my mother said.

"Jesus," my father said, walking into the kitchen.

My mother took the earrings off and threw them at his back. I heard one hit a glass window pane and then half a second later the *clink* of it landing in the sink.

The piano tuner played the keys one at a time. She stood, reached into the piano box. Morning sun slanted through the window and in it I could see specks of dust drifting in every direction. I wondered how many breaths we could take before that dust filled our chests completely.

Another voice on the tape. A brittle voice, the texture of something found beneath deep water and left too long in the sun to dry. The voice told about a birthday party where children sat in a circle and watched a magician pull his own hand loose from his arm. The magician's fingers continued to move as the birthday children passed a piñata bat back and forth through the empty space between the magician's moving hand and the hole of his shirt sleeve.

The man paused and the tape hummed a steady fuzz. When he cleared his throat and spoke again, he no longer seemed to be talking into the tape recorder but off to the side of it somewhere.

"All these years later," he said. "I still have dreams where that hand's left behind. Those fingers down there deep in the cold, dark water still moving, pointing to something far away."

The night I was sent to stay with my grandfather, my mother sat in the living room with the lights off watching a home movie. My father was upstairs packing my clothes into a paper bag. I stood at the edge of the room watching the TV screen. My mother didn't know I was there. In the movie, my parents are younger, both of them crouched on top of the refrigerator calling my name, over and over. When I come into the room I am unsure on my feet, just old enough to walk. I pass beneath my parents, too small to see them there. They put their hands to their mouths so that I wouldn't hear them laugh. I walk out of the room. And then the smile disappears from my mother's face. She climbs off the refrigerator and runs after me, leaving my father on top of the refrigerator alone.

My mother rewound the video and watched it again. Above us, my father's footsteps were moving across my room, packing all the things he thought I'd need.

The piano tuner closed the lid of the piano box when my grandfather came in and I turned the volume so low I could no longer hear the voices.

"I don't know how it keeps going out of tune," she said.

My grandfather sat on the floor beside the map. The piano tuner knelt beside him and traced her finger over the lines he'd drawn.

"You've added so much," she said.

"Finished the cemetery," he said pointing.

"It's red," she said.

"I marked the high ground in different colors," he said. "If you go there, you can still see the statues."

"You never took me," the piano tuner said.

"It's far," he said.

She didn't look up at him, but instead reached over and untied his shoes. My grandfather stood and stepped out of them. The fan turned slow and the peacock feather brushed his shoulder. He reached down to help her up.

"Tell me about the dance hall again," she said.

As he led her to the bed, he told her about the dance floor and the two pianos. How after the dam was complete and the flood-water was coming up through the floorboards a man and his wife stayed behind dueling those two pianos, the pedals splashing water as they played.

The piano tuner got in bed before undressing. She handed her clothes to my grandfather and he folded them and set them onto the piano box before getting in beside her. I'd seen this before. The blankets beginning to move. A bare arm slipping out from beneath the covers and gripping tight to a canopy pole.

I turned the volume on the cassette player back up and listened as the morning light began to change, the shadows cast across the floor grew longer. The voices on the tapes described all the things they imagined still sunk at the bottom.

A train set and the memory of it circling a Christmas tree long after the New Year when the pine needles began to gather in piles on the floor.

A jar of ten-cent baby teeth.

Newspaper photos of an elephant hung by the neck from a railroad crane.

When the piano tuner left, my grandfather was asleep. I climbed down from the attic and tip toed to the map. I bent and traced a finger over the lines the way the piano tuner had.

"It's almost finished," my grandfather said.

I flinched, looked up. He was sitting, running his fingers through his thin hair. Behind him on the wall was a framed cardinal's feather. A single fingerprint left against the glass catching the light.

"How long you been here?" he said.

I stood and tapped a high note with my pinky finger.

"Just now," I said. "I was by the lake skipping rocks."

My grandfather pulled his shirt on but didn't get out of bed. "Bring that here," he said.

I picked up the map and spread it over the bed like a winter quilt.

"See there," he said. "That's the old barn. When I was younger than you it burned. I can remember walking through what was left of it. We picked up barn nails from the ashes. Some of them were still warm."

That night my father called. I stood in the kitchen and watched my grandfather with the receiver pressed to his cheek. He stayed quiet for a long time, picking at a loose scrap wallpaper. Gypsy moths fluttered against the windows. The kitchen sink dripped into an overflowing coffee mug. When my grandfather finally spoke, he said, "Can't always believe the world should be the way you want it to be." And then later he said, "that's the peculiar thing about women."

The next week the piano tuner came again. My grandfather was in town having the radio repaired. The night before, the Braves lost a game they could never get back. And what I knew about love then was that a line drive into center field in the bottom of the eleventh could make a grown man walk out of his own house and throw his radio onto the roof.

The familiar sound of the piano tuner turning the doorknob. The hinges creaking, and the way she shut the door so you couldn't hear it close, only the click of the bolt turning back into place. Her footsteps soft on each floorboard. The smell of her perfume before she came into the room. A scent that always reminded me of the color white. Like new sheets on a summer bed with windows open, a screen door flapping against a door jamb in the breeze.

I was sitting cross-legged in the attic studying the map of the lake and listening the voices on the tapes. Voices that spoke the language of ghosts. My grandfather's map a neat reconstruction of what had once been theirs. The bygone roads, the forsaken homes. In the backyard of one of the houses he'd drawn a pack of dogs crowding something at the bottom of a rain ditch. In the driveway of another house, children waiting their turn to fly a kite, a kite that may or may not fly high enough to stay dry once the dam turns that whole world to water.

She paused at the doorway, the fingertips of one hand barely touching the doorframe. She wasn't carrying her tuning tools.

"He's gone," I said.

She looked up, surprised.

"I know," she said.

She came into the room and I heard the floorboards resist against the small weight of her steps. I took off my headphones and set them on the wicker trunk. She climbed the ladder and I watched her thin fingers, the dark veins and fingernails painted a sunset color.

"He hasn't taken you out there, has he?" she said nodding at the map.

"We walk down there sometimes," I said. "But he doesn't think the boat is ready."

"He hasn't taken me in a long time," she said.

The piano tuner picked up the map and folded it into a square.

"Come on," she said. "Before he gets home."

We crossed the backyard and she found a key hidden beneath an antique clothes iron my grandfather used as a door stop to the garage.

Inside were work benches covered in tools and scrap wood. Hung on the wall were lengths of driftwood that had been whittled into the shapes of fish. A metal canoe was flipped upside down on the ground. The few windows were thick with dust and when the piano tuner flipped on a light, the whole place felt like being underground somehow.

She led me to the far wall and pulled out a wooden box from beneath a work bench.

"We used to take the canoe out," she said. "When we first met. Your grandmother had already passed then, but he was still working to finish the house he'd promised her."

She opened the box and pulled things out, placing them on the work bench.

There were square nails and hinges. A window lock, a baby's rattle so rusted it made a dull sound when shook. A dinner spoon, small lengths of barbed wire, and the metal handle of a hairbrush. There were steel marbles, a doorknob, a broken piece of what the piano tuner said may once have been the wheel of a sewing machine. And there were things neither of us could figure. A set of gears smaller than thumbprints, a spring lost of all its tension. A fish hook bent into the letter P.

The piano tuner untied her necklace and laid it on the table. It was a metal leaf with a piece of string strung through a hole in its stem.

"The first time I came here," she said. "To tune the piano. We walked down to the water afterward and he told me about the town hidden beneath all that water. About the post office and how for years they'd find letters washing up downstream. And the dueling pianos splashing notes as the water rose. The ball fields and the creeks and the mailboxes with flags still raised."

As she spoke, she was rearranging the objects back into the box.

"The next week he called me to come back, said the piano had come undone again. Come undone, that's how he said it. He stayed on the porch while I was inside. When I came out, I could see he'd dragged the canoe to the edge of the lake. He took me out to the center, and I pretended like I wasn't afraid. When he stopped paddling he took this magnet from the bottom of the boat and told me to drop it over the side. It was tied to a rope longer than anything I'd ever seen before. I dropped it and we watched that rope run out of the boat and when it finally stopped he pulled it back up. Brought up mainly trash. Crushed tin cans and pieces of boat motors. But he promised me there were houses down there. That people had left everything they owned running from the rising water. And when I was sure he was lying, he pulled this up."

The piano tuner held up her necklace. I touched it with the tip of my finger and the leaf spun a few times in one direction and then slowed before spinning again the other way. When it stopped, she tied it around her neck and tucked it back into her shirt.

"And then he took us back to shore," she said. "I remember before I left I tried to give him a hug, but he was sweating and he shook my hand instead."

"But he doesn't take you out there anymore?" I said.

"He found out I didn't know how to swim."

We dragged an aluminum canoe across the dew-slick grass toward the edge of the lake. Closer to the water, stones scraped against the metallic underside. There were two paddles in the canoe, a length of rope, the round magnet.

I stepped in first and felt the boat quiver. The piano tuner pushed off the bank with one foot and stepped in all at the same time so that when she sat down we were already moving away from dryland.

The sound of our paddles being pulled through the cool water. The drip of it against my leg, like rain. I thought of my mother. A stormy night. Her leaning against the windowsill in my room as I pretended to be asleep. And between lightning she cracked the window and reached her hand out into the night. When she brought it back in she ran it through her hair and touched my cheek before leaving the room. Her fingertips were damp. Lightning lit again and I held my breath until I heard thunder.

We were far from anything when the piano tuner stopped rowing and spread the map out.

"Somewhere in here," she said.

She handed me the map and scratched her finger on the house where the children were taking turns flying their kite.

She handed me the magnet.

"Hold the rope and drop it over," she said

The first few tries came up empty. The piano tuner would check the map and paddle the boat a few strokes in a new direction. On the seventh try I pulled up a metal toy soldier. The soldier's legs were bent as if riding a horse, one hand fixed between his knees. But the horse was missing. The piano tuner dried the soldier with the tail of her shirt and set him on my knee. We dropped the magnet again but never found another soldier, never found a horse for him to ride away on.

The piano tuner untied the magnet and wrapped the rope into a tight coil.

"I want to see one more thing," she said.

We rowed to the point of a small island. An egret flew low, so close to the water its wings almost touched the mirror image of its own reflection. We were circling to the backside of the island when the piano tuner tapped the side of the canoe with the butt of her oar and pointed the blade.

"There," she said. "Do you see them?"

There were statues standing atop the water. We paddled closer and I saw crosses made of stone floating there. Concrete roofs sheltering the surface of the lake.

The piano tuner paddled slow through the cemetery. Gravestones not tall enough to stand out of the water lingered beneath the surface like pale shadows that rippled as we passed. A virgin mother stood holding a virgin son. Her free hand was palm up toward the cloudless sky.

Something hit the surface of the water in the shadow of a mausoleum roof and I gripped my fingers white around the handle of my paddle, afraid of what had come loose from those sunken graves. The piano tuner saw me laughed.

"Don't worry," she said. "It was a fish. The dead here haven't learned to swim yet."

When we got the canoe back into the garage, my grandfather was in the kitchen talking on the phone. He held up one finger toward us when we came through the back door. The radio was plugged in on the table beside the couch and I could hear the announcer calling out the starting lineup.

The piano tuner walked through the kitchen on tiptoe and soon I heard the soft notes of the piano. I turned the volume down on the radio as my grandfather picked at the kitchen wallpaper.

"Your father says he might be coming tonight," my grandfather said after he hung up the phone. I was sitting on the living room floor. He stood there looking at me. From the bedroom we could hear the sound of the piano tuner tapping the high notes. My father in a car somewhere, his headlights and the darkness out ahead of them. I wondered if he found her in Florida. If he sat alone on the beach and threw his wedding ring into the ocean the way I'd seen it done in a movie.

My grandfather turned the radio back up and we listened to the announcer call the first pitches of the game.

"You took the boat out?" he said.

"I saw a ghost," I said. I felt at the soldier in my pocket but kept it there hidden. "She told me it was a fish."

The Braves threw three strikes in a row and my grandfather slapped the leg of his pants.

"Think they'll win it all?" I said.

"I'm just hoping they don't break our hearts," my grandfather said.

I thought about the voices in the attic. The purse of marbles still hidden beneath a porch board. That missing hand pointing its fingers in the direction of dryland.

My grandfather turned and went to his bedroom. He shut the door behind him and I climbed on top of the refrigerator. The sound of the piano stopped and for a long time it was quiet. I set the toy soldier on the edge of the refrigerator, his legs bent perfectly so that sitting there seemed to be something he was meant to do.

At some point, the sound of the piano's fallboard being lifted and thudding into place. This time the keys weren't tapped, one at a time, the way they were when being tuned. Instead, notes were played. High and low. One chord leading into another. It was a song I had never heard before, a song that might have never been played until that moment and then maybe never again. I imagined the two of them sitting there at the foot of that canopy bed. Her hands atop his showing him how to form the notes and then later, lifting hers away so that he was playing along to the memory of her touch.

When it was over, the door opened and closed again. The refrigerator hummed. My grandfather passed beneath me without looking up. He was shirtless. Sweat gathered in the hair of his chest. He stopped at the sink and filled a glass. He drank it and began to fill it again. Somewhere at the bottom of the lake was a toy horse. I flicked the soldier from where it sat and when it hit the ground my grandfather shut the water off. He set the glass into the sink and turned. The soldier was face down, knees and forehead pressed against the wooden floor as if praying.

My grandfather watched the soldier a long time and then, as if he'd remembered something, he turned, filled his glass and walked back to his bedroom without ever looking up.

The sink faucet was dripping. I climbed down from the refrigerator and left the soldier there on the ground to pray. It was late. I cupped my hand beneath the faucet and let the water pool in my palm. The radio announcer called a strike, and the Braves were up by one in the third. I ran my wet fingers through my hair and turned the radio off. A single note sounded from the piano, almost too quiet to hear.

That night I walked barefoot to the water and watched for ghosts to break the surface. I skipped rocks to wake them, dipped a toe in and wondered if the dead feel cold or warmth or anything at all.

I had never been to Florida, but I knew it was white sand beaches stretching beneath the high, hot sun. Nights when the moon's reflection stretched and quivered out over the dark water, and translucent crabs following the ebb of the tide. My father trying to figure out the geometry of a woman's heart, a science as shifting as the movement of the seasons.

What I'd learned about love was that it drove my grandfather to unplug his radio and throw it on the roof without saying a word. Love that made him loosen the piano strings late Wednesday night and drive into town to have the radio repaired in the morning.

Love that brought the piano tuner back into the house built for a dead wife, and the reason she packed her tools neatly into the leather fold she never forgot to take with her when she left.

Love was the earrings my father bought for another woman and the sound of one of them hitting the glass window pane and love in the silence of the world before that earring landed heavy in the metal sink. Love was home movies watched in the dark and the footsteps across the ceiling above.

The voices on the tape spoke of loved things. Things lost. Things remembered. Things still here but out of reach.

Love like a red feather framed in driftwood.

Love, something to be sorted.

# Nightmare Prayers

I t's 2:00 a.m. and the old man is sleeping. He keeps me up most nights crying out what sound like nightmare prayers to God. I guess something behind his eyelids looks too much like Hell. His words come out tangled up and twisted. I listen to him, lying in bed, scared those dreams will be my dreams one day. The doctor said people in his condition often have trouble sleeping. I didn't tell the doctor that before Mom died, and before his condition, they slept in separate rooms so that she wouldn't wake up with bruises on her arms from where his fists swung at things that haunted his sleep.

She said it didn't happen much. But now, with half his mind gone and the other half going, seems like these fits come on most every night.

When he wakes, the old man says he doesn't remember anything about his dreams, but he's always drenched with sweat and sore from shaking. His bones must remember. You can see it in the way he limps around the place.

It's 2:00 a.m. and the neighbor girl's light comes on. I can see it out my window. Only for a minute and then off again. I pray she's just getting up to use the bathroom. Sometimes her man comes over late. Lets loose whatever anger he found out there in the late hours of the night. Shouting cusses and breaking things the neighbor girl will have to try and put back together when he is gone. He keeps at it until he tires himself out and falls asleep on the couch. Sometimes the light is on all night. Sometimes he doesn't get tired.

The hands on the clock move slow in the shadows, but I don't blame them. They got nowhere to be and no one to help them get there. I try to close my eyes, but the old man is at it again, and these thin walls don't keep nothing secret.

When I was fourteen, he got drunk one night and told me about a girl who used to live in the woods. A girl whose eyelashes grew in long braids down to her waist. I'd heard about her my whole life, rumors told in whispers at school, but never from the old man. He said she showed up the first day of school one year. Rumors spread that the girl was sick, that if you touched her braids you'd catch something incurable. The old man just wanted to see the color of her eyes. He saw beauty in something so strange. But she was gone after a week. Her daddy took her back into the woods because she couldn't see nothing and the other kids would pull at her eyes when the teacher wasn't watching. The old man never tried to stop them, and he always wondered what would have happened if he had. He heard that her father had taught her how to divine sacred ground, how to move slow through the lost parts of the woods and feel for God's breath. And once she got the hang of it, she charged a week's pay to show people where to bury their prayers. She'd even dig the hole for them. And sure enough the following spring they'd come back with prayers answered to the spot she'd marked and see that something beautiful had grown. But one year nothing bloomed, and people claimed the prayers they'd buried hadn't been answered.

The girl cut her braids one morning when snow was thick on the ground and shot herself through the chest. At her funeral, her eyelashes had already started to grow back out. The priest closed the lid of the casket and refused to open it, even for family, because he believed there was evil inside.

For all I know, the old man said, she's buried somewhere with her eyelashes still growing, maybe up toward the sky like trees. Maybe deeper into the earth like roots looking for somewhere dark enough never to be seen.

The old man said her daddy was holding a locked box at her funeral and wouldn't speak to anyone. Must have had those braids locked up in there. Thrown the key somewhere it would never be found. A week later he was gone. Probably drove until the road ended into shoreline and threw that box in the ocean, prayed for it to sink.

Maybe that's what the old man sees when he sleeps. That wild girl cutting her braids and firing a pistol into her breast. A dust of blood being covered by a slow fall of snow.

I check the clock and count off three fingers, three hours until the sun lightens the timbered horizon. In school, they laughed at me for counting on my fingers when everyone else had calculators that ran off sunlight. The old man said he'd never needed a calculator, and that was that. Good enough for me. When I moved back last year, after Mom died, I noticed the old man counting on his fingers, always starting with the thumb, same as me. But now, sometimes it seems like the numbers get lost, and he has to shake out his hand and start from zero.

A few cars pass on the road outside my window. Some of them moving too fast, some moving too slow. All of them moving at a speed that seems dangerous this time of night. I hear a thud from the old man's wall. Sometimes he swings fists. Sometimes he kicks his bare feet. Always he fights back.

I worry I'll walk in there one morning and he'll be dead, lying on the floor. Knuckles bruised and head split open. People will come to his funeral and see what a mess he'd done to himself and whisper to each other that I shouldn't have been the one caring for him, that I couldn't even keep him safe at night.

The girl I was with before I moved home said I was crazy. Said I should put him in a home where people who knew what they were doing could look after him. I told her I wasn't going to lock my own father up in place he didn't know, surrounded by people drooling down their shirts and waiting to die. The next day, I quit my job at the rock quarry and didn't even tell her goodbye. Didn't know she was right for saying what she'd said.

Three more hours, I think, and open a window to let the cool night in. I like the damp on the pillow in the morning, the smell of a new day beginning again. It's only then I can sleep, with the scent of the old man's coffee coming from the kitchen and the birds calling out songs to wake dawn.

The clock is getting closer now. The neighbor girl's light turns on again, and this time for good. Maybe she'll make a pot of coffee, an egg or two. If her man isn't passed out on the couch, she can sit and watch infomercials until it's time for work. His truck isn't out front so maybe he didn't show up. Maybe there isn't a bathroom sink full of broken shards of mirror glass. Sometimes I worry she'll go into work with a busted lip and eyes swollen and bruised. I imagine her telling lies about sleepwalking into a doorframe, her coworkers nodding and waiting until she's gone to exchange knowing glances. She'll hear them whispering and she'll run to the bathroom to cry, the tears coming out red and trailing down her cheeks like braids. The world is turning gray. The old man is in the bathroom running hot water over his stiff fingers. The neighbor girl starts her car and tries to back out of the driveway without bumping the mailbox. She gets too close and pulls forward, turns the wheel and tries again. The sun is coming. Dew is damp on the sheets. Soon I will be able to sleep.

When I wake up, the old man is gone. Fishing. A baitless hook and the child's pole I bought him at the flea market the morning I first found him standing by the pond tossing pebbles into the flat water and waiting for it to still again before tossing another. Used to be you'd get a bite almost every cast in that pond. Not anymore. Now I don't know what's beneath the surface.

The doctor said the old man would have good days and bad days. But good or bad he always leaves the house with that pole and comes back hours later having caught nothing. On the bad days, he has trouble remembering my name and wakes me up to tell me he's going to the big pond to meet Markum Lundgrave. Markum was a friend of his from growing up. He died almost fifteen years ago. On good days, he doesn't say anything to me at all, lets me sleep until the high sun comes through my window.

Today is a good day. I get up and pour what's left of the coffee into a SEE ROCK CITY mug with the old man's name on it. Mom bought it for him years ago, and there are coffee rings inside that don't come out when it's washed.

The coffee is cold, but I've learned to drink it that way. The old man unplugs the coffee maker before he leaves, even on bad days.

I set my half-full mug in the sink and go into his room. The bed is made, sheets tucked tight beneath the mattress. Even with his brain turning to shit he still keeps clean and organized. I open the drawer and remove his shirts and underclothes. I try to keep them creased the way he folded them. His suitcase is in the closet. I fill it, put a picture of him and Mom on top of his clothes, and zip the suitcase shut. In the picture they are standing together, leaning against a railing, the ocean behind them hundreds of feet below. I wonder if he'll remember taking that picture, if he'll open the suitcase and try in vain to remember the woman's name.

Before Mom died, I asked her about the story the old man told me when I was fourteen. She'd heard of a girl living in the woods with braided eyes since she was a little girl. Everyone around here had their own version of it.

"And that's your daddy's," she said. "He had him a girlfriend in high school, thought he was going to marry. Her father was a preacher, and he'd take your daddy out with him to run his bird-dogs. Taught him these prayers to say as they went along. 'Lord bless this earth beneath us lest we walk on unholy ground.' Things like that. Before they graduated that girl killed herself. Your daddy never could figure out why. Blamed himself, I think."

❊

I pull my pickup to the edge of the pond and cut the engine. The old man sees me and nods in my direction. I stay in the cab of the truck, watching him. The tip of his rod is motionless, the surface of the pond as still as a pane of glass. I sit and watch until the truck's too hot and I can't bear it any longer.

"Catching anything?" I say.

"Couple nibbles," he says. He is standing but motions for me to sit in a folding chair beside him.

I can't tell if he recognizes me or is just being friendly.

"Pulled a catfish the size of your thigh out of here couple years back," he says.

I sit down. "Is that right?"

He turns to me. "You remember."

"My eighteenth birthday," I say. "You brought the grill out and Mom cooked them up as quick as you could catch them." I don't tell him it was almost twenty years ago.

The old man reels in the line and spits on the naked hook and throws it back into the murky water. "You ran off soon as it got dark," he says. "And that girl Loren, her uncle brought you home around daybreak with nothing but your britches on. He said he pulled you out of that house while his brother was looking for a rifle, didn't have time to get your shirt."

We both laugh, and I try to keep smiling, but it seems like the good days are harder than the bad ones. Days when his brain snaps back into shape for an hour or two and I think he's back for good, then his eyes start moving quick and he asks me my name again, tells me it's been nice talking with me but his wife and son ought to be home any minute for supper, and that he's sorry, but he's not interested it whatever it is I had come to sell. That I should run along and good luck.

I think about that girl with eyelashes in long braids. I wonder how she knew when she was standing on holy ground. What prayers could she help me say for the old man? And what would grow out of the earth if I said them right?

The old man's hook splashes against the surface of the water and I watch the ripples expand. He lets it sink and the line disappears across the pond. I can see the bruises on his arms where he'd fallen out of bed.

I tell the old man I need to take him somewhere, and he doesn't say much. He reels the hook to the tip of the rod and folds up his chair. He puts both in the bed of the truck next to his suitcase. I see in his eyes that he recognizes it.

"Where you taking me?" he says.

I climb in the cab of the truck and crank the engine.

He gets in and pulls his door shut, but not all the way. The ajar symbol lights up on the dash.

"Door ain't all the way closed," I say.

"Where we going?"

I'm already sweating so I turn the AC on high. He turns it off. I stare at the ajar light and feel his eyes on me.

"Dad, I just can't," I say. "I just don't think I can do it on my own anymore."

The old man turns away from me and pulls his door closed. He rolls down his window. I try to think of something else to say, but it's too hot in the truck and my mind's not working right. I put it in gear and turn the radio to his favorite station. I don't know if he understands any of this. Neither of us says anything. The old man's eyes look angry. The muscles in his jaw are clenched.

After an hour, the old man begins humming along to a John Prine song. The boy in the song wants his daddy to take him back to the green river. The daddy says *son I'm sorry, but it's no longer there.* The old man knows every word. I turn and look and see the anger has left him. He is calm and relaxed, one hand hung out the open window, tapping along to the beat of the song.

"Next anniversary," he says, "I'm taking my wife down to Nashville to see John play the Opry. Already got the tickets, hidden in my sock drawer."

I pull over to the side of the road and cry into the steering wheel. I feel the old man's hand on my back, a hesitant pat, the way you would try to comfort someone crying next to you at the bus stop.

He says, "Everything is going to be okay, fella," and gets out of the truck. I know that when I pull it together and tell him to hop back in he is going to ask me my name.


I stand in the parking lot of the assisted living facility. The old man's fishing pole and chair are still in the bed of my truck. His suitcase isn't. I wonder if I should run back in and bring him his pole. But I already made a scene in there, cried like a boy watching his dog get put down. The old man just watched me wondering who the hell I was. The nurse said I could come back any time, sign him out and take him fishing. When she said this, the old man smiled big and told her that a few years ago he'd reeled in a catfish big as her thigh.

On the way home, I drive through the Depot and get a bottle of Dickel. I take a pull while the cashier makes change. He gives me a cross look but doesn't say anything. He reaches me my change, but I tell him to keep it. I see his arm outstretched as I pull away.

When I get to the pond, there's a good bit missing from the bottle. The sun has already set, but there is a gloam of light hanging onto the horizon. A white pickup passes by slow and stops in front of the neighbor girl's house. I watch it, red tail-lights lit up. A bullfrog splashes the water. I wonder if there's any fish left beneath the surface, or if the old man pulled them all out years ago. The white pickup drives off.

It's almost full dark when I see the pickup come back again. This time it doesn't stop. The neighbor girl's man is inside. He's got the dome light on. I can see him in there, one hand at the top of the steering wheel and a ball cap pulled low over his eyes. He guns the engine just to let her know he's out there. He looks at me when he passes the pond and turns the dome light off. I figure he's going out to find him a barstool somewhere, figure this isn't the last time I'll see him tonight.


It's close to midnight when I knock on the neighbor girl's door. I saw her leave an hour before, but even when you're sure no one's home you still knock. I turn the knob, but it's locked. Around the back of the house, I find an open window. I reach through and feel a sink faucet. There are no lights on inside. I set the bottle of Dickel on the counter and climb through the window. The handle of the faucet catches my foot, and I hear the water turn on as I fall to the floor. I stand and touch the cold stream of water before turning it off.

In the living room, I sit on a worn-out leather recliner and wait in the dark. The house is as quiet as a church prayer. I think about the old man in some new bed, shouting Hell into the shadows. Sweat staining the mattress beneath his sheets. Bones fighting to hold together as he shakes violently until morning. I wonder if the walls at that place are thin like ours, if those other old men and women have their hands over their ears, afraid of the voice they are hearing.

A few minutes go by, or a couple hours. Headlights brighten the room, casting shadows where before there was nothing but darkness. I reach for the bottle and feel that it's empty, lighter now and not capable of as much damage. It'll have to do. The old man once taught me where to hit a man to bring him to his knees. I figure if I close one eye I can see straight enough to know where to swing. The lights go off, and I'm standing in the dark. The floor is swaying to try and tip me over, but I widen my stance and stay upright. The lock turns and the bolt clicks into place. Keys land against a wooden table. High heels clatter onto the floor. The lights come on and I've got one eye open and a bottle neck tight in my fist.

She sees me and stands there trying to figure me out. Doesn't even scream. Seen things like this too many times before. I look to the door to see if she's alone or if he's coming through behind her. She follows my gaze.

"Where he at?" I say.

"Who?" she says.

I wonder if I picked the wrong house.

"That man who comes here to see you," I say. "Drives a white pick up."

The girl's shoulder hunkers beneath some lonesome weight.

"What did he do?" she says.

I point the bottle at the window pane he'd broken out a few nights before, the window she covered in cardboard the next morning before work.

"He done that," I say.

She looks at the window and then takes a small step toward me.

"And I'm sure he done worse," I say. "I'm just hoping to keep him from it tonight."

She sets her purse on the floor and sits on the shoulder of the couch. "I know you?" she asks. Her body is relaxed but her eyes stay sharp and focused on me.

"My old man lives next door," I say. "I've been staying with him the last little bit. Keeping an eye on him."

"Thought you seemed familiar," she says. "Sit down and let me get you some coffee."

I try to form a sentence in my head, but I can't seem to find the right words.

"Left my old man today," I say.

She stands and crosses the room.

"Take your coffee black?" she says.

Coffee's a good idea. Sober me up some in case that son of a bitch shows up and tries to get at her. I fall back into the chair and mumble something that sounds like 'yes, please.'

I hear her take the phone off the hook in the kitchen, hear her pressing the numbers quick. I can't make out everything she is saying, but I get enough to know this was all a mistake.

"...man in my living room...please hurry...1217 Trussle Road..."

She comes back in with two cups of coffee, but I'm already at the door. I know I should apologize, try and explain that I only came to help, that I made a mistake, that she's a good girl and deserves better than to have men showing up at her house when all she wants is to be left alone. I know this is what I should say, but instead I feel my stomach retch, and it's all I can do to make it out to the front lawn. When I'm done, I wipe my mouth on the sleeve of my shirt and hear the door lock behind me. I don't turn around. I pray she keeps it locked forever.

I sit beside the pond and wait for morning. The cops came. I watched them from a bush. They stood in her yard and talked. She stood in the door and kept her arms crossed. Later, when they were finished with her they crossed the street and knocked on the old man's door. No one there to answer. Just an empty house with walls too thin and half a mug of cold coffee in the sink. The cops drove away. Now, all there is to do is wait for morning, when I can get some rest. I hear the birds beginning to wake. The old man is probably already up, running warm water over his sore hands.

As the sun comes up, I lie back and close my eyes. I feel sleep hanging from my eyelids, like heavy braids. The ground beneath me is good ground. Sacred ground, I think. But I don't know if God is listening, and I don't know the words to pray. So I just tell him what I'll do. I'll sleep off the whiskey and drive out to see the old man. I'll take his rod with me and sign him out for a couple hours. I'll bring him to the pond and sit right here and watch him toss that spit hook into the water. Both of us hoping a fish hits it and pulls hard. The rod will bend and threaten to snap. And the old man will remember how it feels to bring something heavy to the surface.

# Acknowledgments

I'd like to thank:

My parents for the years of unconditional support.

Neal Walsh and Drew Jordan. This wouldn't be a book without you.

Everyone at The College of Charleston and the University of New Orleans:

Bret Lott, Anthony Varallo

Barb Johnson, Rick Barton, Joanna Leake

Dan and Danny

Thank you to Hub City Press:

Meg Reid and Kate McMullen, you made this book real.

# Notes

Several of these stories first appeared in the following publications:

"Whittled Bone," *Pembroke Magazine*
"Satellites," *South Carolina Review*
"Nothing for the Journey" (Originally printed as "Asphalt. Pumpernickel. Iron."), *New Limestone Review*
"Rainpainting," *Fiction Southeast*
"Jaima," *Bat City Review*
"Beneath Dark Water," *Greensboro Review*
"Dryland," *Arts & Letters*
"Nightmare Prayers," *Baltimore Review*

— C. MICHAEL CURTIS —
SHORT STORY BOOK PRIZE

THE C. MICHAEL CURTIS SHORT STORY BOOK PRIZE includes $10,000 and book publication. The prize is named in honor of C. Michael Curtis, who has served as an editor of *The Atlantic* since 1963 and as fiction editor since 1982. This prize is made possible by an anonymous contribution from a South Carolina donor. The namesake of the prize, C. Michael Curtis, has discovered or edited some of the finest short story writers of the modern era, including Tobias Wolff, Joyce Carol Oates, John Updike, and Anne Beattie.

**RECENT WINNERS**

*Sleepovers* • Ashleigh Bryant Phillips (2020)

*Let Me Out Here* • Emily W. Pease (2019)

PUBLISHING
*New & Extraordinary*
VOICES FROM THE
AMERICAN SOUTH

HUB CITY PRESS has emerged as the South's premier independent literary press. Focused on finding and spotlighting new and extraordinary voices from the American South, the press has published over one-hundred high-caliber literary works. Hub City is interested in books with a strong sense of place and is committed to introducing a diverse roster of lesser-heard Southern voices. We are funded by the National Endowment for the Arts, the South Carolina Arts Commission and hundreds of donors across the Carolinas.

**RECENT HUB CITY PRESS FICTION**

*Child in the Valley* • Gordy Sauer

*The Parted Earth* • Anjali Enjeti

*The Prettiest Star* • Carter Sickels

*Watershed* • Mark Barr